Praise for *Allie's Bayou Rescue*, Book One in the Princess in Camo Series

"Allie's Bayou Rescue is an awesome book to read together as a mom and daughter! We love how real it was about the obstacles we face as girls—but not without a God who cares for us in our struggles, pursues us, and knows EXACTLY where we are going. And has it all under control—especially when we don't!"

ELISABETH AND GRACE HASSELBECK, TV PERSONALITY AND DAUGHTER . . . AND DAUGHTERS OF THE ONE TRUE KING!!!

Finding Cabin Six

Other Books in the Princess in Camo Series

PRINCESS IN CAMO
Finding Cabin Six

By Missy and Mia Robertson

With Jill Osborne

ZONDERKIDZ

Finding Cabin Six
Copyright © 2018 by Missy Robertson and Mia Robertson
Illustrations © 2018 by Mina Price

This title is also available as a Zondervan ebook.

Requests for information should be addressed to:
Zonderkidz, 3900 Sparks Dr. SE, Grand Rapids, Michigan 49546

Library of Congress Cataloging-in-Publication Data
ISBN 978-0-310762546

Art direction: Kris Nelson
Interior design: Denise Froehlich

Printed in the United States of America

18 19 20 21 22 /LSC/ 10 9 8 7 6 5 4 3 2 1

"If a man has a hundred sheep and one of them gets lost, what will he do? Won't he leave the ninety-nine others in the wilderness and go to search for the one he has lost until he finds it?"

LUKE 15:4

There are only a few places in your childhood that you know truly helped shape who you grow up to be. Mia and I could have never written a series without including this special place. It contributed to my growth in Christ, and now it has contributed to my children's. A big thanks to the founders, directors, staff, and volunteers who have made Camp Ch-Yo-Ca what it is. I'm so thankful to be able to share this amazing place with everyone through this super cute book!

—Missy

To all the awesome people who have helped make Camp Ch-Yo-Ca the happiest place on earth! #100AcresOfHoly.

—Mia

To Missy and Mia—thank you for allowing me the privilege to work with your family to see the Princess in Camo series come to life! And to all the summer camp workers out there— you're some of the toughest and most faith-filled people I know. Never give up—you're changing lives for eternity!

—Jill

"Where's Betsy?" Katherine stuffed the last of her dirty camp laundry into her duffle on the top bunk and flicked her flashlight beam over and around seven empty beds.

"She's bathing, of course," Emma said. "You would think that girl was getting ready for the prom, instead of . . ."

"Shhh." Katherine put her finger up to her lips. "Don't *ever* say it out loud."

Emma covered her mouth and whispered, "I'm sorry, Kat."

"Don't fret about it." Katherine climbed down the wooden ladder. "Just help me with her bed roll, please."

Katherine and Emma moved several stacks of clothes off Betsy's bottom bunk, refolding and stuffing it with her bedding into an oversized suitcase. Katherine's fingers fumbled with the tiny metal zipper pull.

"I can't believe we're actually doing this." Katherine grabbed a hand towel from her bunk and wiped her clammy fingers.

"Me either," Emma said. "I'm just happy we're all sleeping in the tree house tonight."

"Yes. That little victory was a Godsend." Katherine lifted Betsy's suitcase off the bed and groaned at the weight of it.

"Emma—we must keep this to ourselves. The fewer who know the better."

Emma held up three fingers. "A cord of three strands is not easily broken."

Just then, a hint of lavender wafted into the cabin, and

9

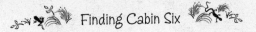

Betsy—the third strand—opened the screen door and poked her head in.

"Are we all ready?" Betsy squealed. "I'm sure I'll never again in my entire life be involved in such a delightful mission."

Katherine grabbed her duffle off the top bunk. "And you won't be involved in this one if you don't get your two-ton suit-case out the door right now."

CHAPTER 1

Necessities

"Duct tape, rope, scissors, hanging vines, monkeys . . ." I scratched my head and scanned the shelves and other flat surfaces in the bedroom I share with my cousin, Kendall.

"Can you think of anything else we need?"

Kendall pulled some super glue from her desk drawer and then crammed a purple ukulele into the medium-sized suitcase we had set aside for "camp essentials."

"There." She sat on her bed, scrunched her lips together, and rested her fist on her chin. "What about flower garlands?"

I pointed to my teeny, white, poof-ball dog, Hazel Mae. She and Kendall's black miniature poodle, Ellie, were playing tug-of-war with the garlands.

"Good luck getting those away from them in one piece."

Kendall jumped off her bed and ran toward the dogs.

"Ellie! Drop!"

At the sound of Kendall's command, Ellie and Hazel Mae disappeared out the door with the garlands.

Kendall threw her hands up in the air. "We need those if we plan on being cabin champs again this year."

"I'm sure there are more in the boxes downstairs. I saw some inflatable birds and geckos too."

Kendall sat back on the bed and crossed her arms. "There are a million boxes stacked up down there."

My family—who had been living with Kendall's family for a long nine months—was packing to finally move into our

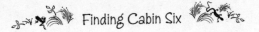

newly-built, allergen-free home on a brand-new street in our neighborhood—Timbuktu Court.

Our move-in date was planned for next Monday—two days after we were scheduled to return from our week at summer camp.

"Come on." I grabbed Kendall's hand to tug her off her bed. "I'll help you dig through the boxes."

But we didn't move, because Kendall wrapped me up in a tight hug.

"I don't want you to move, Allie."

I laughed and tried to pry her arms from around me. "Yes, you *do*. And I'll only be five minutes away."

At the top of the stairs, we ran into my mom, who was carrying an overloaded laundry basket. She pushed us backward into our room and dumped the load of socks and underwear on my bed.

"I hope you girls intend to pack clothes and toiletries too." She glanced down at the suitcase with the twenty monkey eyes staring back at her.

"What in the world do you need *those* for?"

"Mom—everyone knows you need monkeys at camp."

"We're creatin' a rainforest environment," Kendall said. "We're goin' for cabin champs three years in a row, and décor is one of the top things they judge."

Mom began sorting socks from the mound. "And what if you girls *aren't* in the same cabin this year?"

I put my hands on my hips.

"That's *not* gonna happen."

Mom shook her head. "Well, okay. I'm just preparing you for the possibility—I don't want to hear you griping if you end up separated."

"We *have* to be together. This is our last week as roomies!

Plus, we've written our cheer and everything." Kendall grabbed a couple of socks off the bed and swung them around like pom-poms.

"We're the best, and we will thrive, 'cause Jesus is alive in Cabin Five!"

Mom raised her eyebrows. "And how do you know you'll be in Cabin *Five*?"

"We've worked our way up," I said. "We're the oldest now, so we rule. That's all."

"But there are *lots* of girls your age, and last time I counted, there were only nine camper beds in Cabin Five. So, clearly *someone* isn't going to rule."

Kendall plopped the cheer socks back on the bed. "Yeah, too bad for them."

Right then my phone rang. The caller ID popped up a name: Madison Doonsberry.

I sighed. "It's Madison . . . again. She probably needs more packing advice. She's never been to a summer camp before."

"Tell her we could use some more monkeys," Kendall said.

Fiery redhead Madison Doonsberry and I got off to a rocky start last November when her family moved into my old house. She seemed to hate me for some reason, so I secretly referred to her as "Mad-girl," and tried to avoid her—kind of like how I avoid eating peanuts—to *survive*. But then, through a painful set of circumstances, God showed me that Madison didn't need someone to make fun of her or avoid her—she needed someone to care. And after a *lot* of prayer, I decided to try that—but slowly, and in small doses. Then, Madison found out she and I were both going to be at the same camp the last week in June, and she'd been calling me at least three times a day since Wednesday.

So much for small doses.

I poked the "answer" button on my phone and put her on speaker with me and Kendall.

"Hey, Madison. Are you still packing?"

A little puppy yelp came from the speaker.

"Petunia, stop chewing on the curtains!"

Petunia is Madison's golden retriever puppy.

"Allie, how many pairs of shoes should I bring? Petunia's chewed up most of mine."

I laughed. "That's fine. Chewed-up shoes are the best ones to bring. They're gonna get wet and dirty anyway."

"Petunia!"

Things went quiet on the other end of the line for a minute. Then Madison returned, out of breath.

"Wet *and* dirty? Why?"

Kendall laughed. "Camp. That's why."

"But it's a *Christian* camp, so there's less dirt, right? Doesn't everyone just sit around and make sweet crafts and sing hymns?"

"Ha! That's the funniest thing I've ever heard, Madison. Hang on a minute, I have to jot that one down in my journal."

"Don't tease me, Allie Carroway—and be truthful. How much dirt are we really talking about here?"

"Madison—there's dirt *everywhere*. In fact, bring dirt-colored clothes. And lots of socks."

"How many exactly?"

"At least three pairs for each day. And two pairs of shoes for the week. One to wear while the other dries out."

"Oh, yuck!"

Silence on the other end again.

"Madison? Are you still there?"

"Yes. I'm hugging Petunia and trying not to cry. Allie—I'm not sure I'll survive this week."

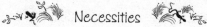

"Sure, you will. You're a bayou girl now, remember?"

I heard a loud sigh on the other end.

"Yes, I remember. In fact—it's my daily nightmare. Allie, will you help me when I'm at camp? I'm nervous. And I don't understand all that Christian stuff either. The packing list says I'm supposed to bring a Bible, and I don't even have one. Well, there is one on a stand in our living room. But it's the size of a small suitcase."

"I'll bring you a Bible."

"Oh, thank you, thank you, thank you!" Madison then began talking to her puppy. "Petunia, I'm going to miss you so much!"

"Okay, well . . . bye, Madison."

I hung up and lay down on my bed. I clasped my hands, raising them toward the ceiling.

"Kendall, *please* pray—with all your might—that Madison Doonsberry is *not* assigned to our cabin."

Kendall shook her head. "Nuh-uh. Lately, every time I ask God for somethin', he says no. I think *you* should ask instead."

"And *why* shouldn't Madison be in your cabin?"

Mom had returned with more laundry and glared in my direction.

I propped myself up on my elbows. "She's just not the camper type, Mom. And that means she'll be clingy and whiny. This is my last year at middle-school camp, and I don't want to spend it babysitting Madison Doonsberry."

"Well, it sounds like *you* have a little selfish streak going on." Mom set the laundry basket beside me on the bed and pulled an envelope from the top of the load. "According to this, it may be your last year at camp, *period*." She handed it over to me.

I opened it, and pulled out a letter to my parents from Lindsey Roth, our close family friend, and director of Camp 99 Pines.

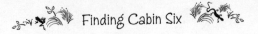

Dear Camp 99 Pines Alumni,

We are eagerly awaiting your arrival next week to celebrate the Camp 99 Pines' 50th year anniversary! Enclosed you will find your tickets to the gala—to be held under the stars on everyone's favorite recreation field two. It's going to be a fabulous night, with three hundred in attendance!

Attached you will find a parking map for Friday evening. Also, for those arriving a day early, we are offering lunch and a tour of the camp at noon—when our middle-school students will be in session.

The next part of the letter made my heart hurt.

As I wrap up this letter, I am compelled to ask you to pray about the future of Camp 99 Pines. Founder and owner—Audrey Gables—is suffering from Alzheimer's Disease, and has been admitted to a local care facility. Her son, Patterson Gables, has put the property up for sale, and a housing developer has already offered a sum that is over the asking price—one that we on the camp board cannot match at this time.

Our camp is booked for the summer, so we will continue to operate, but if nothing changes, our last week as a Christian camp will be the week of August 9th. Until then, we are . . .

Trusting in the God of
all Hope,
Lindsay Roth
Director, Camp 99 Pines

"Till all the lost have been found."

"Allie—your face! What's wrong?" Kendall jumped up off her bed and grabbed the letter out of my hand. "What does it say?"

"It says that the camp is up for sale," Mom said.

"For sale? Why?"

I pointed to the shocking paragraph.

"Audrey Gables' son wants to turn it into a neighborhood, I guess."

"A neighborhood? We've got plenty of neighborhoods!" Kendall stomped one foot on the floor. "Camp 99 Pines is historic—they can't sell it!"

"Can the Carroways buy it?" I turned to my mom. "We've got money from doing the show, right?"

My whole family stars in a reality TV show called *Carried Away with the Carroways*. It all started when I was about seven, and it focuses on our life in the Louisiana bayou—particularly my dad and uncles and their duck hunting escapades.

"Do we have enough to buy the camp?" Kendall looked over at Mom, who was now sitting on my bed, matching up pairs of socks.

"Maybe," she said. "But owning a camp is a huge undertaking. And something tells me that this situation is a lot more complicated than someone else simply buying the camp."

"What's complicated?" I said. "We buy it, and it stays a Christian camp."

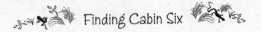

Mom took the letter from Kendall and shook her head. "It says right here that Audrey's son, Patterson, is in charge now, and it appears he has other interests. Maybe he's not even a believer."

"With parents who own a Christian camp? That impossible."

"It's possible in any family, Allie," Mom said.

"Well, either way, I think the Carroways should pay a visit to this Patterson Gables person." I balled up a few socks and threw them in my suitcase.

Mom's eyes opened wide. "Allie, I think that's enough socks."

"Yeah, but I could be mucking around in the mud this week, looking for ways to save the camp."

Mom pointed her index finger toward my chin.

"Listen here, girl. You're going as a *camper*, not a crusader. Got that? Let the grown-ups figure this out. You just pray."

I didn't change my expression at all.

"Allie . . ."

"I'll pray," I said.

"And take *good* care of Madison. Put yourself in her shoes. How would you like to be treated as if it were your first year at camp?"

I nodded. "Yes, ma'am." I reached into my top dresser drawer and pulled out more socks. "She'll need these."

A long pause. Then Mom continued.

"You'll be out in the bayou with snakes and alligators. No mucking, sneaking, hiking, peeking, or even *thinking* about lurking around where you don't belong."

"Yes, ma'am."

She took a deep breath.

"Okay, then. I'm going downstairs to call Mamaw and Papaw and make sure they know about the pending sale of

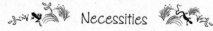

the camp. Then I'm meeting your dad at the new house for the walk-through with the builder. Do you want to come and see your room?"

"Nah. I'll wait till move-in day."

"Can we *not* talk about that sad topic anymore?" Kendall looked like she was going to cry.

Mom walked over to Kendall and kissed her on the forehead.

"My sweet niece, it's been lovely living with you and your family. But we Carroways need our space." Then she exited our room and was soon down the steps.

I looked over at Kendall.

"Mamaw and Papaw, and *both* our moms and dads met at Camp 99 Pines."

Kendall shot to her feet.

"So, if it closes, we may never meet *our* future husbands."

I giggled and threw a balled-up sock at Kendall. "I thought you were going to marry Parker."

Parker is Madison Doonsberry's twin brother. He's much less complicated than Madison. Cute too.

"Ah, yes, Parker! You're right. Then let's save the camp so *you* can meet *your* future husband, Allie. He might even be there *this* summer."

I rolled my eyes. "Hmm, yeah. And I'll have six whole cabins of stinky, middle-school, creepy boys to choose from. It's not happenin'."

"Did I hear you girls talking about *me*?"

My cousin—Kendall's younger brother Hunter—poked his sweaty head in the door. His blonde curly bangs were stuck to his forehead.

"Oh, hey, Hunter. We weren't talking about you. You're family, so you're exempt from the 'creepy' category."

Hunter stepped in and stuck out his chest. "I feel honored.

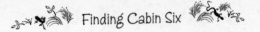

Hey—do you think I'll get made fun of if I bring my dinosaur pillowcase to camp?"

"Oooooh. Don't do it!" Kendall gritted her teeth.

"Oh, please!" I stomped my foot on the ground. "It's a Christian camp, people! Bring whatever you want, Hunter. They'll adjust."

Hunter grinned. "Good. I'll throw it in." Then he disappeared.

"Kendall, we can't let Camp 99 Pines be turned into a boring neighborhood." I checked my phone—9:30 a.m. It was almost time for our Saturday morning "Donuts-in-the-Split" meeting with all our preteen cousins. I gave Kendall a determined stare. "Text the cousins and tell them to get to the Lickety Split, lickety split!" I laughed. "We'll all be at camp for a whole week. There's gotta be something we can do! We just need to come up with a plan."

Kendall's thumbs started whipping out texts.

"Somethin' tells me I need to pack more socks."

CHAPTER 2

Allie Carroway— Camp Crusader

It didn't take long to gather all the cousins in our clubhouse—a tree house that we named the Lickety Split. Lola, Ruby, and Hunter joined Kendall and me on the patio by 9:45.

"Allie, we were packing for camp. What's so urgent?" Lola—who was sporting a yellow button-down shirt and fashionable army-green camp shorts with daisy piping down the sides—smoothed her hand through her shiny brunette bob with the pink streak.

Ruby—her younger sister by only a year—leaned on the twisted branch railing around the patio and stared out toward the rolling hills in our neighborhood, her harvest orange braid hanging in front of her right shoulder. She was wearing jeans, of course, and last year's Camp 99 Pines T-shirt.

"I'm actually happy for the break. Lola has her whole closet spread out all over our room. I needed some fresh air."

"Is this urgent meeting about my dinosaur pillowcase?" Hunter asked.

I lead my cousins through the front door, and we all took our regular seats in the Lickety Split. Kendall and I sat on the large, tan beanbag, Ruby and Lola plopped on the brown over-stuffed love seat across from us, and Hunter leaned back, all peaceful-like, in the orange Adirondack chair in the corner.

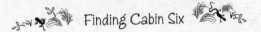

"Camp 99 Pines is up for sale," I said. "And the owner wants to sell it to a housing developer."

Lola shrieked. "No! I haven't met my husband yet."

Kendall crossed her arms. "Lola, that is *not* the point. This is about people findin' Jesus."

Lola bit her lip. "I suppose you're right. It's just a Carroway tradition. One I don't want to break."

"Then let's figure out how to save it," I said. "We're clever and smart. And we're on TV."

"And that helps us how?" Ruby asked.

I tapped my fingers on the beanbag. "I'm not quite sure yet. But remember, we *did* raise all that money at the school carnival with the show's help."

"But your mom said that Patterson Gables might not want to own a Christian camp." Kendall got up and started pacing around. "So even if we raised enough money, he'd probably sell it to someone else anyway."

"It's just so depressing," Lola said. "To think that Camp 99 Pines won't exist anymore."

Ruby sighed. "That's my favorite place in the whole world."

"And I haven't even been there yet," Hunter said.

We all just sort of sat there, moping. And then we heard a familiar whistle outside.

It belonged to Uncle Saul—our Papaw Ray's younger brother.

"Hey—Carroway kids! Y'all up there?"

I jumped off the beanbag and shot out to the patio.

"Hey, Uncle Saul! Whatcha doin' in our neighborhood?"

"Lookin' for trouble. You know of any?" He stroked his long gray beard and smiled up at me.

My cousins joined me outside on the patio. Kendall whispered in my ear, "Should we tell him? Maybe he can help us come up with a plan."

"Nah. He can't keep a secret."

Hunter rushed to the railing and shouted down before we had a chance to stop him. "Uncle Saul, did you know they're selling Camp 99 Pines to a housing developer?"

Uncle Saul put his hands out to both sides of his body, and his eyes popped open wide.

"Sellin' the camp? Ain't gonna happen! God'll stop that nonsense."

Then he walked away, whistling. Calm as could be.

Kendall narrowed her eyes and crossed her arms. "He seems a little too relaxed, don't you think?"

Uncle Saul stopped and turned to look back at us.

"No need to worry, kids! That camp'll be around for another 99 years."

"Yeah," I said to the cousins. "He must be up to something."

CHAPTER 3

A Hopeful Word

Eventually, you have no more room in your suitcase, so you cram in the last monkey, say a prayer that the zipper won't break, and head to camp.

It was Sunday, right after we attended the early morning service at church, and Aunt Kassie had volunteered to drop us off at camp while the rest of the family celebrated our departure.

At least I think they celebrated. I'm sure I heard Uncle Wayne yell as we all waved goodbye out the car windows: "Woohoo! Got rid of 'em! Let's go eat! More food for us!"

Twenty minutes into the trip, Lola pulled a crumpled list from her backpack.

"I hope I didn't forget anything."

She checked her paper list, and I went over the list in my brain. And as we rounded the corner on Route 99 that goes by Mamaw and Papaw's house, it hit me.

"I forgot to pack an extra Bible for Madison!" I tapped my Aunt Kassie on the shoulder from the back seat of the SUV. "Can we please stop at Mamaw's?"

My Mamaw Kat collects a *lot* of things—and books is at the top of that list. She's filled many rooms in her house with books for us kids. My favorite "book" room is a building on the side of the house that she calls the Prayer Barn. I knew it would hold just the right Bible for Madison.

"Yes, let's stop!" Hunter rubbed his belly. "I'm hungry!"

Aunt Kassie shook her head. "You kids." She never said

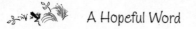

whether she would stop or not, but fifteen minutes later, she pulled up to the house. Mamaw was outside, throwing a tennis ball for her dogs, Andi and Barney.

Mamaw put her hands to her cheeks.

"This day just keeps gettin' better and better!" She came over to hug us all as we got out of the SUV.

"What're y'all doin' here?" She checked her watch. "Shouldn't you be on your way to 99 Pines? Are ya hungry? I baked some cookies last night."

"I knew it!" Hunter ran up to the porch, threw open the screen door, and disappeared. Lola and Ruby followed.

"Great," Kendall said. "There go my chances for gettin' a bottom bunk. Might as well have a cookie, then." And off she went too.

"Mamaw, can I borrow a Bible for Madison? She's never been to a Christian camp before and she doesn't have her own Bible yet. I was going to throw an extra one in my suitcase, but I forgot."

Mamaw put her hand on her heart.

"Madison Doonsberry? She's goin' to Camp 99 Pines with y'all? That's the best news I've heard *all* week."

I sighed. "If you say so. I'm a little worried about what's gonna happen with her there. I'm not sure I really trust her yet, after that whole dog show disaster."

Mamaw put her hands on my shoulders.

"I'll tell you what's gonna happen. That little girl's gonna find out just how much Jesus loves her—and then you'll see a beautiful change in Miss Madison Doonsberry." Mamaw gestured toward the Prayer Barn. "You can borrow any Bible you like."

My Mamaw Kat is the most caring person I know in the whole world.

My goal was to *try* to be caring, but Madison had done me wrong in the recent past, almost getting me fired as Student

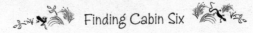

Project Manager of the Bark Fest Carnival and Dog Show—our school's year-end fundraising event.

"Thanks, Mamaw." I climbed up the small hill on the side of the house, opened the screen door, and then pushed on the creaky wood one to get into the Prayer Barn. The familiar scent of books and cedar filled the air and reminded me of the hours I had spent sitting on the comfy brown sofa reading about Moses, Joseph and his brothers, David and Goliath, Joseph, Mary and Jesus, and taking peaceful breaks looking out the windows at the Ouachita River.

"Let's see, what Bible would be the best one for Madison?" I ran my finger along several book spines as I wandered around the bookshelves, and then stopped on a lavender one that said, "Holy Bible." There was something about the look of that one. It was pretty, but a little roughed-up. Kinda like Madison.

"I don't think I've ever seen you before," I said to the Bible as I pulled it from the shelf. I opened the cover. It was old, all right. And on the front page, it had some scribbled handwriting:

```
Dearest Katherine,
     In these pages, you will find everything
you need for this life and the life to come.
The Lord cherishes you. Never forget that!
                    Sincerely,
                    Audrey (Luke 15:4)
```

"Allie-girl, did you find what you were lookin' for?" Mamaw entered the Prayer Barn, and her eyes lit up when she saw the book I was holding.

"Oh, my, that's a treasure there."

I held the Bible open so she could see the first page.

"Is this *you*?" I pointed to the name Katherine.

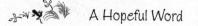

Mamaw nodded. "Yep, that's me. Not many people call me that anymore, though."

"And who's Audrey?"

Mamaw smiled.

"Audrey Gables. She was my Sunday School teacher for about . . . hmmm . . . seven years, I think."

"Is this the same Audrey Gables who owns Camp 99 Pines?"

Mamaw sat down on the sofa. "One and the same. You know, *she* was the one who shared the Good News about Jesus with me. I think I was about nine when I asked Him into my heart. And then Audrey gave me this Bible to take to camp when I was in high school. It was the very first year Camp 99 Pines was open, and she and her husband Quincy were *so* excited." Mamaw leaned back into the sofa cushions and looked out the window. "It was a sad day when Quincy passed, and I'm heartbroken to hear that Audrey's comin' to the end of her life. She was a shinin' light in mine."

I closed the Bible and handed it to her. "I'll take a different Bible for Madison. You wouldn't want anything to happen to this one."

Mamaw took the Bible in her hands and shook her head. "It's not going to do any good sittin' on that old, dusty shelf! The only good Bibles are the ones that get used." Mamaw flipped through the pages. "Let's see, I dropped this Bible in the mud, my friend Emma spilled hot chocolate on it, and if I remember correctly, I even left it outside once on a picnic bench and the sprinklers got it! Yep"—she flipped over to the book of Exodus—"here's the ripply pages to prove it." She held it out to me. "Take it, and if Madison wants, she can keep it. I'll be prayin' that it brings her some hope."

"Allie! Are ya comin'?" Kendall pounded on the screen door of the Prayer Barn. "We gotta get to camp and start decoratin'!"

27

I closed the Bible and held it to my chest with both arms. "Thanks, Mamaw."

Mamaw smiled, stood, and gave me a hug. "Hey, maybe I'll see ya on Friday when I'm out there for the reunion gala."

"That would be great! I'll ask if I can come over and say hi." I opened the squeaky screen door and stepped out, heading for Aunt Kassie's SUV.

"Oh, hey, Allie-girl. Can you drop somethin' off for me to Miss Lindsey? She was askin' for some pictures that show camp history, and I've got a whole scrapbook full of 'em."

"Sure, I'll take it." I followed Mamaw over to the house. And then a thought hit.

"Mamaw—by any chance, did you know Audrey Gables' son, Patterson?"

Mamaw stopped in her tracks.

"Did I know *Patterson*? Of course!" She scrunched up her nose. "He was a smelly little creep."

"A *what*?"

Mamaw put her hand over her heart.

"Oh, I'm sorry. That's a rude thing to say."

I laughed on the inside.

"I only called him *that* when he was in junior high. He started smelling much better in high school." Mamaw put both hands on the sides of her mouth like she was going to tell me a big secret and whispered, "I even dated him for a couple of weeks."

My mouth dropped open.

"You *dated*?"

"Yeah. But then I found out that he wasn't *really* interested in following Jesus. He was just fakin' so I'd go out with him. So, I broke it off! That stinker—trying to close the camp now. We'll see about that!"

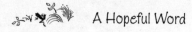

"Wow, Mamaw. You're a real mystery lady sometimes."

"Oh, honey, you don't know the half of it."

She chuckled and then led me into the house and to the living room bookshelves, where she dug out a green scrapbook filled with yellowed pages of photos. She placed it carefully in a plastic bag, and handed it to me. I wanted to stay and ask her more questions about Audrey and Patterson, but the cousins were waiting, I had monkeys to hang in Cabin Five, and I had a treasured Bible to give to a girl I was *trying* to care about all while hoping and praying she would be in a different cabin—away from me.

CHAPTER 4

Roster Woes

We did to Aunt Kassie what we do to every driver who has ever driven us out to Camp 99 Pines. We deserted her at the car with the luggage so we could run for the rosters.

The cabin rosters are posted on the bulletin board in the middle of camp, right next to "the box,"—a square wooden platform with three steps up on all four sides—that functions as our meeting place before every meal.

I couldn't see the bulletin board at that moment because it was being crowded by a huge group of kids—all trying to get a glimpse of their names and cabin assignments.

I ran toward it anyway. I was sure I could squirm in or flip-flop my way to the front.

As I neared the back of the crowd, a ruffled redhead emerged from the scuffle.

Madison.

She was bleary-eyed and looked shell-shocked, but when she spotted me, she grinned.

"Oh, Allie! Thank goodness, you're here! I have *no* idea what to do next."

"What cabin are you in?" My stomach churned as I gritted my teeth.

"We're in cabin four," she said. "Do you have any idea where that is?"

We're?

"Daddy has my luggage over at the truck. Parker's still in the fray." Madison pointed to the crowd by the bulletin board.

We're?

"Allie, are you okay? Are you sick?" Madison nudged me in the shoulder, which popped me out of the shock zone.

"Uh, yeah. I'm okay. Just adjusting to the camp air, I guess."

"Did you bring your inhaler? You look pale."

Madison knows about my many allergies. She's even *made fun of me* over them in the past, calling me Allie-Allergy.

"I'm fine. Let me just check the roster first, and then I'll help you, okay?"

I'll escort you to Cabin Four and then I'll take my rightful place in Cabin Five. Jesus is alive in Cabin Five.

"Well, okay . . ." Madison glanced over toward the pushing mass of middle-schoolers. ". . . but you may not escape without injury. I'll meet you over by . . . uh . . . I don't know where *anything* is. I guess I'll just wait . . . here."

She looked a little pathetic, standing there all alone, while kids wheeled suitcases and hauled duffle bags right by her, as if she were a mailbox or a small tree or something you don't normally acknowledge.

Try a little harder to care, Allie.

I shrugged. "C'mon, I'll help you find your cabin."

"You might as well bring your bags. It's your cabin too."

This girl *had* to be imagining things.

"Are you *sure*, Madison? Because I'm supposed to be in Cabin Five this year."

Madison shook her head. "Your name was two lines above mine, listed in Cabin Four. Carroway, Carroway, Doonsberry. Ruby's in with us. Kendall and Lola are in Cabin Five."

My heart sank.

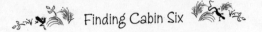

How will we split up the monkeys? And WHO *thought it was a good idea to separate the Carroway cousins anyway?*

"Well, hello, Miss Allie." A familiar, loving voice sounded behind my back. It belonged to Lindsey Roth.

Sweet, family friend . . .brilliant camp director . . .and cabin roster maker!

I turned, and tried to plaster on a smile.

"Hello, Miss Lindsey. It's nice to see you."

"Welcome back to camp, Allie. It's going to be a great week!" Lindsey held her arms out to give Madison a polite hug. "And you must be Madison Doonsberry. I met your dad a few minutes ago and he pointed you out. You were climbing through the crowd, but I could see your gorgeous head of hair in the mix."

Madison pinched a curl and smiled. "It's nice to meet you, ma'am."

"Now, I know it's your first time ever coming to summer camp. Don't you worry, we'll take good care of you. I made sure you are in a cabin with the best camp tour guide around. Allie will show you the ropes."

My ears started buzzing.

Miss Lindsey, how could you do this to me?

"Lindsey!" Tammi Lakewood—who's been our camp nurse every summer since I've attended, shouted from the nurse's hut steps. "We need you over here! I've got a kid with meds but no parent release."

Lindsey turned and then excused herself.

"Gotta go! It's always a little chaotic at the beginning of camp. Madison, if you have any questions, ask Allie. She knows everything there is to know about surviving in this place."

But I don't know how to survive in Cabin Four without Kendall!

Lindsey took off at a slow jog, leaving me alone with Madison again.

"I'll meet you over by our truck," she said. "Daddy has my bags out and ready to go."

I glanced over at the raised, black pickup truck that had the logo for Madison's dad's fishing-and-law-advice reality show, *Lunker Law*, painted on the side. It dwarfed the three pink suitcases sitting in front of the black grille.

Three suitcases, Madison?

I walked backward, rubbing my face and trying to erase the last few minutes from my mind.

I retrieved my *one blue* suitcase and sleeping bag from the dusty ground next to Aunt Kassie's SUV, and headed toward Madison and the girls' village.

CHAPTER 5

Bag Boy to the Rescue

"How far *is* it?" Madison pulled and tugged, and then stopped to adjust and rest every five steps. Dirt and pine straw jammed under the wheels of her suitcases to the point where she had to drag them—and it proved to be too much for her. It's a good thing I was dragging her big one. Mine was in my other hand, with my sleeping bag stacked on top.

"Where's your sleeping bag, Madison?" I asked, as I adjusted mine so it would be more secure for the next five steps.

Madison wiped her forehead with the back of her hand.

"Oh, I didn't bring one. I much prefer sleeping with sheets and a big fluffy comforter."

No wonder she had three suitcases!

"Would you ladies like some help?" A tan, muscular boy came trotting over toward us. His perfect, light-brown surfer hair ruffled in the breeze.

Hey, wait a minute . . .

His azure blue eyes met mine, and I practically dropped the luggage.

He smiled. "Hi."

I see you still have your dimples.

"Hi." I barely managed to squeak that out.

"Do you remember me?"

I shifted my eyes to the side to see what Madison was up to. She was unzipping one of her bags and fishing her hand in after something, not looking at us at all.

Good.

"Yes." I cleared my throat. "Nathan, right?"

Nathan—the boy from California—the one who had given me a bag of unexplainable, but wonderful items in the Dallas-Fort Worth airport back in November—put out his hand to shake mine.

"Nathan Fremont. I believe you have my headlamp."

I gulped.

Yes, I do. I keep it on my nightstand at home. And, oh, yeah, I brought it with me to camp because it's one of my most treasured possessions.

"Hi." I held out my hand to shake his. It was easy to do— since now I was really shaking.

Nathan shrugged. "Your brother dared me to give up summer surf camp and come to the bayou instead. So here I am. He told me you'd keep me safe from the alligators."

My oldest brother Ryan is Nathan's eighth-grade science teacher in Santa Barbara, California. I would deal with him later.

A fair, freckly hand waved in my peripheral vision.

"Hi! I'm Madison Doonsberry, Allie's friend." Madison walked up to Nathan and smoothed her hair out of her face.

Nathan grinned. "Doonsberry, huh? Dude, I think your brother's in my cabin."

Madison made a funny face.

"Did you just call me 'Dude'? That's funny. You aren't from around here, are you?"

Nathan laughed. So gentle. And sweet.

"I'm from Santa Barbara. It's on the California coast."

Madison raised her eyebrows. "You left the sunny beaches of California to come to Jesus Swamp Camp? What—did you lose a bet?"

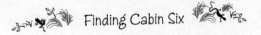

Nathan laughed again, unruffled by Madison's insult.

"Allie's brother is my science teacher. And he *did* kind of dare me. But really, ever since I saw this place on *Carried Away with the Carroways* I've wanted to come and check it out."

Madison narrowed her eyes.

"You must have sand in your brain."

Nathan laughed. Again.

"That's a definite possibility."

Who are you? And why aren't you smelly and creepy like the rest of the middle-school boys?

Nathan reached over, grabbed the handle of my suitcase with the sleeping bag stacked on top, and then picked up one of Madison's suitcases by the handle, lifting it off the ground.

"Point me in the right direction."

I started walking toward the girls' village.

"You can only go as far as the sign. No boys are allowed past that."

Nathan looked over at me and smiled. My cheeks felt like they were going to catch fire.

"Well, I'm sorry I can't help you take these all the way, but I'm happy to lighten the load a little."

We reached the famous tree with the sign that says: "NO BOYS ALLOWED PAST THIS POINT." It also has lots more wooden signs nailed to it that say G1, G2, G3, G4, and G5, with arrows pointing every which way toward the matching cabin.

"What cabin are you in, Nathan?" I asked.

"Cabin Six."

Of course. Top of the food chain in the boys' village.

"Hunter's in my cabin too. I haven't met him yet, but I saw his name on the roster and recognized him from the show."

"Oh, good. He'll have you laughing all week. But whatever you do, don't make fun of his dinosaur pillowcase."

Nathan smiled. "I would never do that."

We stood there for an awkward moment, and I suddenly realized that Madison was still several yards back, dragging her suitcase. Nathan ran to her, scooped it up, and brought it to the tree.

"Okay, ladies. I better go find my home for the week." Then he turned to me. "See you at lunch?"

My heart fluttered way too hard, and I blurted out way too loud, "Sure!"

And then he took off.

"Wow," Madison said. "Was that kid for real?"

I watched as Nathan Fremont hiked back toward the box and the bulletin board, turning the corner toward the boys' village.

"It doesn't seem like it," I said.

But I *hope so.*

CHAPTER 6

On the Floor in Cabin Four

The good thing about Cabin Four is that it is near the bathroom. That's the only good thing about it.

While all the other cabins have steps that lead up to a wide porch, Cabin Four sits at ground level, providing a welcome entry for snakes, lizards, rats, and other pesky creatures that like to sneak in whenever someone opens the door.

"Oh, good, we don't have to climb steps!" Madison pulled her suitcase up and over the doorjamb. She dropped the handle and it thudded onto the wood floor. I'm sure ten lizards came crawling in after her.

"It looks like everyone's already moved in." I scanned the rectangular-shaped room. It had five bunks. Two against each of the long walls of the cabin, and one on the shorter back wall. Almost all the beds held sleeping bags, still rolled up, with suitcases placed next to them. I spotted Ruby's denim duffle bag on the first top bunk on the right side. Her sleeping bag was rolled out and her pillow was tucked inside. She's always quick to adjust to a new environment.

A note was taped to the ladder at the side of her bed.

```
Allie,
    Went to Cabin Five to help hang monkeys.
See you soon.
                        Ruby
```

What a peaceful little letter. I didn't sense one bit of frustration from Ruby about being stuck in Cabin Four.

"Allie, I think this bed is broken!"

Madison sat on the empty bottom bunk under Ruby's bed, bouncing up and down in the middle of it. Then her bottom-half sank down, and it looked like she was sitting in an innertube—her legs flailing wildly.

I reached out to grab her hand and lift her off the mattress. Then I folded it back to reveal a huge hole in the wood that had either rotted out or been eaten by some wild bayou creature.

"That's horrifying," Madison said. "I can't sleep there."

I scanned the room again, and found that the first top bunk on the left was empty.

"Do you mind sleeping on a top bunk?"

"Can snakes get up there too?"

"Yes. But it takes them a little longer."

"Oh, my. Whatever." Madison began to climb the ladder. She reached up and pounded her fist on the mattress, sending a poof of dust rising to the ceiling.

She coughed. "I'm going to die here, Allie! Or catch some dreaded disease. Where's our counselor? I want to file a complaint."

I checked out the bottom bunk under Madison's bed. A purple sleeping bag was laid out—with a Camp 99 Pines fleece blanket folded up and placed neatly over the pillow. There was a note on that bed too. I picked it up and read it out loud.

My name is Bliss.

    I am your counselor, and this is my bed.

    Please do not sit on it, touch it, or move anything on it. Especially, don't touch my pillow! Thank you kindly.

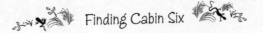

P.S. One of the bunks has a hole the size of Texas in it. If you're the girl who ends up there, drag the mattress down and sleep on the floor for tonight. We have quality people working on the problem.

"What kind of a name is Bliss?" Madison scratched her head.

"All the counselors have camp names. Redwood, Echo, Hawk, Ember—names like that. Most of them return every summer. But I don't know a Bliss. She must be new."

"She sounds rather particular about her bedding." Madison smiled. "I like her already."

Madison climbed down the ladder, walked over to her biggest suitcase, unzipped it, and pulled out a purple quilted comforter with white tassels attached along the edges.

"Will you help me make my bed, Allie?" She continued to pull out some lavender and white sheets, and a white fleece blanket. Then she held up a little stuffed pillow with a picture of a golden retriever on it. Madison squeezed it next to her cheek. "I miss my Petunia already."

My eyes started to roll, but I caught myself and stopped, since Madison was looking right at me. Her golden retriever puppy Petunia is a real cutie. The director of our local animal shelter helped me get the dog for Madison to replace Madison's other golden retriever that had passed away right before she moved to our town. It was kind of a peace offering—a *try* at caring. And Madison and I had been getting along better ever since.

Maybe if her bed is made she'll go up there and take a nap or something and leave me alone.

"Sure, I'll help."

I took the sheets out of Madison's hands, then noticed

there was some weird feathery, fluffy stuff still at the bottom of her suitcase.

"What's that?" I asked.

"Decorations! You told me that the judges like a well-decorated cabin, so I brought feather boas and some pink and purple scarves and garlands. We can be the 'God's Princess Cabin.'" She pointed to one of the other suitcases. "I brought tiaras and matching pillowcases for all of us."

No, no, no! This isn't happening!

"We can imagine that *this* is a castle." Madison kicked the old bunk ladder. "Okay, we'll *really* have to use our imaginations." She pointed out the door. "Out there—the whole dirty, swampy, nasty, germy camp—that's our moat. I only wish we had a drawbridge to pull up so that the slimy creatures in the moat can't reach us."

Now, the idea of a moat was fun. But I would have liked to be on the *other side* of it. In Cabin Five.

Madison dug some more in the suitcase, pulled out a piece of purple cloth, and handed it to me. "Here you go, Allie. I took a chance that we would be cabinmates!"

I unfolded the cloth. It was a pillowcase that said, "God's Princess, Allie."

I swallowed hard. "Thanks, Madison. That was really thought-ful." I unzipped my suitcase, took out the small pillow I had crammed in there, and pulled the new pillowcase over the brown pillowcase that I use specifically for camping. Because it's the *color of dirt.*

"There." I turned the pillow around so Madison could see. "It's nice." I tried to produce a genuine smile.

Madison jumped a little. "I brought rugs too!"

"Rugs?"

Madison pulled out three or four rolled-up shag rugs. One of them said "Welcome to the Palace."

"This we can put in the center of the cabin . . ." She brought out a welcome mat that was a little less fancy, but pink all the same. "and . . . *this* one is for wiping our shoes on. I got the darkest pink possible since you promised dirt."

I chuckled.

Then she took out some frosty pink bubble lights. "We can hang these all around on these little temporary hooks I got. Daddy bought me battery packs for the lights since I figured we wouldn't have electricity. Won't these look pretty at night?"

Yes, I will enjoy looking up at those from my bed—on the floor.

Next, she pulled out a little pink lamp—with battery pack, of course. It was like her suitcase was Mary Poppins' carpetbag.

"Did you leave room for socks?" I joked.

Madison pointed to the third suitcase. "All my clothes are in there."

I nodded, and began to climb the ladder to put her fitted sheet on the mattress.

The next ten minutes were somewhat comical. It's not easy to make up a princess bed on a narrow top camp bunk. That is why *normal* people use sleeping bags at camp! Madison stood on the ladder and threw the flat sheet and comforter toward me, and I pushed myself against the wall of the cabin and did my best to tuck things in. At one point, I backed too far toward the foot of the bed and my legs flopped overboard.

"Allie! Be careful! I can't afford to lose you." Madison reached out her hand and grunted as she helped pull me back up. When the bed was all made, Madison handed me the pink lamp, and I placed it on the little shelf at the head of the bed and clicked the switch on the battery pack, turning the light on.

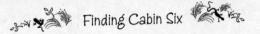

"Perfect!" Madison said. "It almost makes me forget I'm at camp."

At that moment, a bell rang.

Madison frowned. "What's that?"

I smiled. "It's lunch."

CHAPTER 7

The Bell Still Rings... For Now

Madison held her hands over her ears as we made our way through the girls' village and back to the box.

"How long is it going to clang like that?"

I laughed. "Until someone takes the dinger out and hides it somewhere."

She stopped and gave me a funny look. "Takes the dinger out?"

"Yeah. It's a tradition that one of the cabins sneaks out at night, takes the dinger, and leaves a clue about where they hid it. That makes Johan super grouchy, because if he can't figure out who did it by the end of the week, that cabin earns fifty-million points."

"Who's Johan?"

"He's our activities director. Scruffy-looking guy with wild brown hair. He wears camo pants and pretty much the same wrinkly camp shirt all week. You'll be seeing a lot of him."

"Is he Dutch?"

"Huh?"

"I just thought with the name Johan . . ."

"Oh! No, he's from around here. Johan is just his camp name. He says it means champion. Johan hates to lose; therefore, he will hunt down every possible clue to find the cabin members who take off with the dinger."

We made it to the box with all the kids who had arrived

45

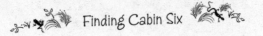

at camp so far. Kendall, Ruby, and Lola saw us and came running over.

"Where did you go after we left my mom at the SUV? I thought we were all headin' to the rosters." Kendall's eyes were wide, conveying thoughts I knew she couldn't say out loud with Madison there.

"Did you see my note?" Ruby smiled. "Cabin Five is all decorated and ready to go." Then she turned to Madison. "Welcome to Camp 99 Pines."

Madison grinned. "Thanks. So far I haven't been bitten by anything."

"Wait till you go in the bathhouse," Kendall said, and Lola poked her in the side with her elbow.

"Hey!" Hunter and Madison's brother Parker ran over to join our little group. "We made it to Cabin Six! Top of the food chain! And we're going with a dinosaur theme, so my pillowcase is perfect." Hunter gave me a thumbs-up.

"But dinosaurs are extinct," Kendall said. "Not a great mascot for winnin' if you ask me." Lola shoved her elbow in harder this time.

Kendall grunted. "Hi, Parker."

Parker pushed his hands into his jean pockets.

"Hi, Kendall."

"I have a question," Madison said. "Why are there six cabins in the boys' village and only five in the girls'? I mean, I only saw signs for five, right?"

"Yep," I said. "The girls only have five. And nobody really knows why."

"There are *stories*," Lola wiggled her eyebrows up and down.

"But they're all just made up to scare us." Ruby gave her sister the stink-eye.

"I love scary stories!" Hunter said.

Just then, Johan leaped up on top of the box and turned on the bullhorn.

"Welcome, campers! You look like a hungry bunch, so we're just gonna eat now, and wait until later to tell you all the rules of camp, when everyone is here. How's that sound?"

We all clapped.

"Let's bow our heads and have someone thank God for the food." Alec, a boy I recognized from the last two years, stepped up to the box and said grace. Then we followed with the tradition of singing the Doxology:

> *Praise God from whom all blessings flow;*
> *Praise Him all creatures here below;*
> *Praise him above ye heavenly host;*
> *Praise Father, Son, and Holy Ghost.*

I glanced over at Madison in the middle of singing. It was clear she didn't know the words, so she was looking down at her feet as she drew circles in the dirt with her shoe.

"Ladies first!" Johan yelled, and we streamed into the mess hall. The familiar aroma of pizza filled the room.

Kendall took me by the elbow and pulled me aside.

"Allie, I've been thinkin' about a solution to our cabin assignment problem."

I frowned. "I'm so bummed. I can't believe Miss Lindsey split us up."

"I know! But hey, there are these two girls—Natalie and Olivia from Kentucky. It's their first time here, and they don't care about the whole Cabin Five thing, so I was thinking that they might be willing to switch cabins with you and Ruby. What do you think?"

"Uh . . ."

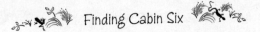

As I thought about that, I looked around at the cabin signs that were glued to lanterns and sitting in the middle of each table. Another tradition at Camp 99 Pines is that cabinmates sit together at each meal. How were the Carroway cousins supposed to sleep *and* eat away from each other for a whole week?

"Okay, yeah," I said. "That's a good—"

"Allie! Oh, *there* you are." Madison held a tray with two plates, each with a slice of cheese pizza, a salad, and a bag of chips on it. "I got your lunch for you. And I met Bliss! She's serving in the food line. I introduced myself and told her all about our princess theme, and she *loves* the idea! I feel *so* much better now, knowing you, Ruby, and Bliss are in my cabin."

I just stood and stared at Kendall.

Madison continued, "So, I guess we all eat at the same table too? This is so fun. I'll see you over there."

Madison practically skipped over to the Cabin Four table.

Kendall gave me an intense stare. "So, do you want me to talk to Natalie and Olivia?"

What should I say, God?

I thought about that huge hole in my bed, and how this could be my last year *ever* at Camp 99 Pines. I thought about how I love the rainforest and hanging monkeys *so much more* than I love tassels, tiaras, and feather boas. I thought about how when I get home I'm moving out and won't be sharing a room with Kendall anymore. It seemed like an easy decision.

But then I remembered what my mom said:

Make sure you take good care of Madison.

And what Mamaw said:

That girl is going to find out how much Jesus loves her—and then you're gonna see big changes in Miss Madison Doonsberry.

And as much as I *wanted* to move cabins, I just couldn't do it.

I cleared my throat. "Kendall, I'm sorry, but I think God wants me to stay in Cabin Four."

Kendall's eyes filled up. "But, Allie, it's our last year."

Then *my* eyes filled up. "I know. But we've been living together in the same room for nine months. You're sick of me, and you know it."

Kendall blinked and a tear fell. "You're right. And I know you're sick of me."

I nodded.

"Are you *sure* God wants you in Cabin Four? 'Cause Jesus is alive in Cabin Five."

I nodded. "I'm pretty sure He can be alive in Cabin Four too."

Kendall sighed loudly and rolled her eyes up to the ceiling. "Ugh! This is *so* uncomfortable!"

I laughed a little. "I know. Hey—maybe we'll be on the same team for Survivor Day."

Survivor Day happens sometime during the week. They never tell us when. We just have to be prepared. Teams compete against each other in crazy events that take the strengths of all the members working together to win.

Oh, no. Madison's going to have to participate in Survivor Day! I hope she survives.

I reached out and put my hand on Kendall's shoulder. "You've got Lola."

Kendall shrugged. "Yeah. But I wanted *all* my cousins together."

"Me too. But we'll be okay. It's only a week. Maybe there's some important reason we're separated."

Kendall raised her opened hands to the sides of her face. "I can't imagine *any* good reason for that."

CHAPTER 8

Boy Rules

I sat and ate cheese pizza with the girls in Cabin Four. They were nice and they all seemed put-together—kind of like their luggage I had seen in the cabin before coming over. I already knew Ruby and Madison—who sat on either side of me in the enclosed patio portion of the mess hall. The other six would take a while to get to know, but their nametags said they were Hayley, Julia, Ashley, Brooke, Shelby, and Kayla. And finally, just as they were calling us up for seconds, Bliss showed up.

"There you are! My Cabin Four girls!" Bliss placed her overflowing salad plate on the space next to Kayla and stretched her arms wide from side-to-side. She wasn't big, but she was sheer muscle. Like one of those Olympic gymnasts who can hold herself on the balance beam with the muscles of one toe.

"Welcome to Camp 99 Pines! I'm so *sorry* I wasn't there to greet ya'll when you got into the cabin." Bliss sat down. "Okay, which girl got the messed-up bed?"

I raised my hand. "If you're referring to the one that has a hole the size of Texas, that would be me."

"Allie Carroway. I am so sorry!" Bliss shook her head. "I know you don't know me, but I feel like I know you, since I've been watchin' your show for years!" Bliss's eyes shifted over to Ruby. "And dear Ruby, I just love you!" She placed both of her hands over her heart.

Bliss sat down, and her long platinum-blonde side bangs fell and covered her left eye.

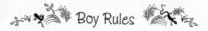

"Did y'all wash your hands in the tub and use hand sanitizer? Because that's what's gonna save us this week, ladies." She held up an index finger. "That, and not touching each other's pillows. Did y'all see my note?"

Madison finished chewing a bite of pizza and swallowed. "Yes, we saw it, and I totally agree. Pillows are for faces—nothing else."

Bliss smiled. She picked up her fork and stabbed multiple pieces of crispy lettuce. "We are just gonna have the best time! I can't wait! Do y'all know there's a waitin' list to be a counselor at Camp 99 Pines? They *finally* called me. I've been prayin' for y'all for three years! Oh, man, God's gonna do some great things, you'll see!"

The rest of Bliss's curly hair was shoved up into a stretchy, buff-headband thing, and some of it poked up and spilled out of the top. Seemed the perfect thing to do with camp hair.

"Where'd you get all those veggies?" Madison pointed to the radishes, artichoke hearts, peppers, and beets that were in Bliss's salad.

Bliss stuffed a bite in her mouth, chewed, and then swallowed. Then she put a finger to her lips. "Don't tell anyone. I have a special counselor food line. I'm allergic to cheese, which makes me allergic to pizza. I'm also allergic to milk, ice cream, ranch dressing—pretty much everything in the camper food line." She gestured to me. "You can relate, right, Allie? One peanut and you're a goner?"

I glanced down at the little pink wrist pack that travels with me everywhere since it carries my inhaler and Epi-pen. Yeah, I could relate. I was sure I would have to visit the special food line for campers a few times this week.

"You mean you can't eat mac and cheese?" I blurted out.
Bliss shook her head. "Not a bite."

"I couldn't live without mac and cheese."

Bliss laughed. "And I couldn't live without peanut butter."

I smiled. "Then I guess we're food opposites."

Bliss chewed a little more, then swallowed. "I guess so. But I'm sure we'll be great cabinmates anyway. Wow—Carroways in *my* cabin! Who would have thought . . ."

Yes, who would have thought? I thought I'd be in Cabin Five.

I glanced over at the girls' Cabin Five table, and saw that their counselor was one I knew—Ember. And of all the counselors I'd met through the years—she was the most relaxed and my favorite.

Bliss went on. "You wanna know somethin'? My great aunt was a camper here the first year it opened. I'm tellin' ya, girls, this is a special place, with a capital S!"

Bliss took a big bite of radish, and while she gnawed on that, I had a thought.

The first year it opened? Could Bliss's aunt and Mamaw have met each other?

"Bliss, did you know that the camp is up for sale?" Ruby's eyebrows were drawn together and she looked like she could barely spit those words out.

Bliss dropped her fork. "What? I don't know anything about that! I just got here last night. I live in Texas, and my flight was delayed by bad weather, so I missed the orientation meeting. How can it be for sale? Who's gonna buy it?"

The girls in Cabin Four were all leaning in now, and wore expressions of shock while they tore off bites of pizza and chewed.

"Well, maybe someone will buy it and do some upgrades." Madison ripped open her bag of chips. "I'm sure things haven't been improved since your aunt was here, Bliss."

I had to laugh to myself, since I know that my family helps

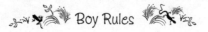

with upgrades every year. In fact, just last fall, they were on a work crew that expanded the craft building, which used to be an enclosed room, and made it a covered outside venue, with ceiling fans and shelves so that everyone has a place to put their crafts.

What does this girl expect? A five-star hotel? This is camp!

Kayla, a tall girl with super white teeth and long, dark brown hair, spoke up. "Hey, see that boy over there? I think he's looking at you, Ruby." She pointed over to the boys' Cabin Five table, where one of the smelly creeps had his head turned, looking right at Ruby. He waved, and then his friend came over to our table!

"My friend likes you," he said to Ruby. "He says you're his favorite person on *Carried Away with the Carroways*. He wants to know if you want to hang out with him during free time today."

Ruby wiped her mouth with a napkin. "I'm sorry," she said. "Tell him that I appreciate the invitation, but my personal rule is 'No love at camp.'"

I practically choked on my pizza. Ruby has a way of cutting right to the chase.

Bliss pointed at Ruby. "That, my dear, is one GREAT rule! Let's make that for our whole cabin, shall we? What do you say, girls?"

"I'm down," Hayley said.

"Oh, yeah, I've got bigger things to worry about." Julia threw her napkin on the table.

"Boys just break your heart," Brooke hit her chest with her palm.

"And I only love my dog." Madison stuck out her bottom lip.

"And we need to stay focused on God and his plan for us this week. So, what do you say we all stack hands on the Ruby Rule?" Bliss stood and put her hand out. The rest of us girls

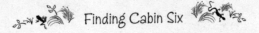

did, too, but as soon as we had our hands out, Bliss pulled a tube of hand sanitizer out of her pocket and began squirting some for each of us.

"Rub it in good," she said. "You're all gonna thank me mid-week when everyone else starts pukin' and you don't. Trust me!"

We rubbed. Then we stacked hands again.

"Okay, NO LOVE AT CAMP, on three."

We pushed our hands down, counted to three, and then yelled, "NO LOVE AT CAMP!"

It caused quite a stir. The kids sitting near us started laughing. I turned to look for the Cabin Six boys. They were a few tables down, but Nathan Fremont was right within my sights, and he was staring straight at me.

And then he winked!

Before my hand sanitizer had even had a chance to dry.

CHAPTER 9

The Last Camper

After lunch, everyone returned to their cabins for a decorating session. Ours was challenging, because we had to work around Redwood, longtime Camp 99 Pines handywoman, and her new assistant this year, Snowball. Redwood and Snowball had arrived in response to a work order, and they hauled with them an electric saw, a long extension cord, hammers, nails, and some old scraps of wood with writing and carvings all over them.

"Allie Carroway, are *you* the one with the broken bed?" Redwood pulled back the mattress, grabbed a piece of the broken wood, and ripped it out of the frame. She inspected it, sniffed it, and tossed it out the front door of the cabin.

"Doesn't look like mold or termites. I think that piece of wood just got tired of camping and gave up."

Snowball grabbed one of the wood scraps that she had brought in and laid it over the hole.

"We may need a couple of these boards to cover this huge hole," she said. "You see, girls, this is how I chose my camp name. Little jobs seem to 'snowball' into big ones around here."

"It was easier to fix things before the spending freeze and we had to find scrap wood to use," Redwood said.

"Spending freeze?" Bliss grimaced. "I hope they don't skimp on the soap."

Redwood laughed. "Oh, no, they won't freeze the budget on supplies for the kids. Just on the maintenance stuff right now

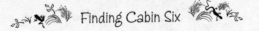

until we find out what's going to happen to the camp. I mean, I get it. Why fix a cabin that might be torn down at the end of the summer?"

I put my hand to my throat. "They wouldn't do that, would they? These cabins are part of my childhood history."

Redwood worked to untangle her extension cord that stretched all the way from the bathhouse. Then she hooked up the saw.

"If Mr. Patterson Gables has his way, this whole place will be demolished. So, for right now, Allie, you'll be sleeping on a piece of history. These scraps are part of some old benches that used to be up the hill. But don't worry, we inspected them to make sure they're free from insects and mold."

Bliss put her hands on her cheeks. "So, the rumor's true? The camp is for sale?" She closed her eyes and raised one hand in the air. I think she was praying.

"I'm afraid so," Redwood said. "But God's gonna come through, you'll see."

Redwood moved us all out of the cabin while she and Snowball replaced the old broken boards with the "new" old bench boards. Bliss dismissed herself to the supply room to get some tape to hang our decorations. The rest of us waited in a little huddle, next to the bathhouse.

A couple of minutes later, Kendall bolted out holding her nose.

"I forgot the air freshener spray! Allie, how come you didn't remind me?"

"Air freshener?" Madison looked surprised. "That wasn't on the packing list. Why do we need air freshener?"

Julia laughed. "Let me see, forty-five girls using the same five bathrooms all week? You do the math."

Madison coughed. "Ugh. I will not go in there, then."

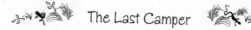

"Your only other choice would be to dig a hole out there," Hayley said, and she pointed to the most wooded part of Camp 99 Pines, which is located just beyond the girls' village. "But you might run into the old hermit lady, Zola Simms."

"Don't talk about that," Kayla said. "I heard that story last year and it freaks me out."

"Who's Zola Simms?" Madison just *had* to ask.

"Oh, please, can I tell it?" Kendall jumped up and down.

"You might as well, and get it over with." I rolled my eyes.

Kayla dismissed herself to go sit on a stump a few yards away. She put her fingers in her ears and started singing, "La, la, la . . ."

The other girls from Cabin Four, along with me, Kendall, Ruby, and Madison, formed a close circle and leaned in.

Kendall began: "Madison, you know how you asked earlier why there isn't a girls' Cabin Six?"

Madison's eyes got wide. "Yeah."

"Well, when the camp first opened, there *was* a Cabin Six."

Madison nodded. "I figured there had to be."

"Yeah, and it was full that year, one counselor, and nine girls—one being a girl named Zola Simms."

"Go on . . ." Madison said with a skeptical tone to her voice.

"The girls in Cabin Six could do nothing but argue all week. And they complained about everything—the food, the dust, the lizards, the smelly bathrooms . . ."

"I-I can relate to that," Madison said.

"Well," Kendall stepped back, looked both ways, and then returned to the huddle, "this made their counselor—Smiles—very upset. After all, her name *was* Smiles, and no one had been smilin' all week. So, she asked the *one* girl who was the most positive—Zola—to go on a walk with her, to pray and

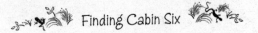

ask Jesus to work in the hearts of the other girls during the last campfire talk."

"We have campfire talks every night where a speaker teaches from the Bible," I filled Madison in.

"Got it," Madison said.

Kendall pointed to the thick woods. "And they went in *there* for their walk."

The girls all turned their heads to look out at the thick forest.

Kendall continued. "The next thing that happened was *so* horrible that none of the senior staff *ever* talks about it. We only know because certain counselors will tell the tale to campers who are brave enough to handle it."

"What happened?" Madison wrung her hands and cracked a couple of knuckles.

"Smiles fell in a gopher hole and broke her ankle."

"What? Why don't they talk about *that*?" Madison crossed her arms. "Seems like that would be common around here."

Kendall brushed off the comment. "Not that part. The next part."

"Oh."

"Zola ran back to the girls' village for help. And when she got there, she saw that Cabin Six was engulfed in flames!"

"I'm out," Brooke said, and she joined Kayla on the stump.

"I told you it was scary," Kendall said. Then she grabbed her stomach and pretended to be overcome with emotion. "I can't go on. Allie, would you finish the story?"

I had been a part of many retellings of the Zola Simms tale, so I went along. "Zola heard the screams of her fellow campers inside the cabin. 'I'm coming!' she yelled. And she went in."

"She went *in*?!?" Madison's hand flew to her mouth.

Man, she's really buying this.

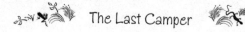

"Yes. She went in seven times, to be exact. And each time, she dragged out a girl—saving her from certain death. By this time, the rescue crews had arrived, and the chief yelled from his truck for her to stop. 'Zola! Don't go in! We have everybody!' But Zola turned and yelled, 'NO! I have to get the last camper!'"

I stopped for a minute to take a deep breath. After telling the story so many times, I had to shake my head to remind myself it wasn't true.

"Zola ran for the cabin, despite the chief's warnings. And when she was only steps from the door, flames broke through the roof and windows. An explosion rang out, and the cabin collapsed—right in front of Zola's eyes."

A few of the girls were clutching their throats now. I went into full drama mode. "'The last camper! I have to save her!' Zola's shrieks rang out, and echoed for miles around. And then . . . Zola Simms ran out into the piney woods, never to be heard from again."

"That's a horrible story!" Madison yelled. "Now I know why Kayla and Brooke are sitting on the stump."

"Yeah, it's pretty intense," Shelby said.

"Well, it's important for everyone to know . . ." Kendall breathed in deeply, "that no girls were lost in the cabin fire that night. Zola *thought* there was one more in there, but the whole time she was in the bathhouse, takin' a shower."

"It pays to be clean, I guess." Madison wiped her sweaty palms. "But did they ever find Zola and tell her the good news?"

Kendall shook her head. "Nope. She's still out there. Much older now—a lonely hermit. Sometimes you can see her in the shadows, rustling through the bushes, always looking for the last camper."

Madison shrugged. "Who's the last camper?"

"Anyone Zola finds out in the woods, walking alone," I said.

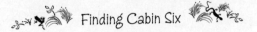

"So that's why I told you not to go out there," Hayley said, "even to go dig a hole."

"Oh." Madison looked in the direction of the woods. Then she turned her head toward the bathhouse.

"I may just hold it all week," she said.

The hammering noises finally stopped, and Redwood and Snowball emerged from Cabin Four.

"Safe to go in now," Redwood said.

"And you won't fall through your bed," Snowball added. "Would you like us to move your mattress back up?"

"Nah. These girls can help me. Thanks for coming so quick so I don't have to sleep with the spiders and snakes on the floor."

"Ha!" Redwood said. "They can crawl up—you know that."

Madison turned white. "That's it, I'm calling Daddy to come get me."

Oh no, you're not leaving, Madison Doonsberry. I'm stuck here in Cabin Four, so you are too.

"It'll be fine, Madison. We spray for spiders and snakes every night."

She sighed. "Oh, that's a relief! I didn't know there was a spray for that."

Ruby laughed. "Are you talking about the prayer spray?"

I smiled. "Yeah." I nudged Madison with my elbow. "It's something we made up a few years ago. We spray our hairspray on each other's heads and say a prayer that God will keep away all the spiders and snakes. Get it? Hair spray . . . prayer spray?"

Madison gave me the squinty eyes. "Does it work?"

"Well," Ruby said, "we've been coming every summer and we're still alive."

"And our hair looks really good in the mornings," I said.

Madison stared like she was in the middle of deep thoughts.

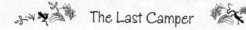

"Okay, I'll try it." She held her index finger up in the air. "First spider or snake I see—I'm calling Daddy."

I chuckled to myself. The staff at 99 Pines wants us to focus on God and each other during the week, so they collect our cell phones, and there are no phones anywhere for campers to use. So, the only "Daddy" we can contact is our Heavenly Father. Which always works for me, since I have a relationship with him. I wasn't sure what Madison was going to do about that.

Lord, help Madison find you this week. I know you've been searching for her.

CHAPTER 10

Mystery Bed

I'm back with the tape!" Bliss paraded through the door with all kinds of girl-colored duct tape. Pink camo appears to be my life even here at camp.

"Let's get this place all spiffed up, beautiful and clean. Our first inspection will take place while we're at dinner. Ducky and Glitch are very picky!"

Ducky I knew. She's been one of the lifeguards for a couple of years now.

"Who's Glitch?" I asked.

"She's our new head of the tech department."

I nodded. "Should we be alarmed by her camp name?"

"Well, y'all shouldn't worry, since you have no technology this week," Bliss said. "But the office staff could be in serious trouble."

Hayley ripped open a bag of candy and dumped it on her top bunk in the back of the cabin. "I'll write a nice note and leave a pile of chocolate."

I turned to Madison to explain. "Bribes aren't encouraged in the Bible, but they are at camp."

"Whatever works!" Madison reached down and tried to lift my mattress off the floor. "Can I help you make your bed?"

Wow, she wants to help?

"Sure. Let me check it out first, for sturdiness."

I jumped up and landed on my backside—right where the hole used to be.

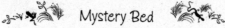

"Whoop! It's as hard as I remember."

I stood, and turned to inspect the old bench wood. Snowball was right, it was a piece of history—with all kinds of words carved in. I bent at the waist and ran my fingers over the old carvings.

"This is really cool. I wonder how old this piece of wood is?"

I leaned in closer, to read the words, names, and phrases.

The first name I saw was Jesus. Appropriate for a Christian camp bench.

The next phrase was a Bible Scripture passage. Luke 15:4. This one I knew well, since it's the Camp 99 Pines motto. Camp 99 Pines is situated at the end of Highway 99, but the number 99 has another meaning. It refers to a story Jesus told about a shepherd who has 99 sheep safely in the fold, but chooses to leave them and go look for one sheep that is lost. And that's how Jesus is. He never stops going after his children—no matter how far they wander away from him. That's why Miss Lindsey always signs her letters with, *"Till all the lost have been found."*

I smiled and said a little prayer for Madison again, and then I noticed some more names on my new bed.

Mary, Barb, Judith, Carolyn.

The names had letters and numbers next to them in parentheses. Mary (G2), Barb (G3), and Judith (G5). I figured that must have stood for the cabins they were in.

Awesome, Judith! You made it into the top cabin. You did better than me!

But then there was another name. Kat (G6).

G6?

"What are you looking at, Allie?" Madison had joined me and poked her head in to see the writing on the bed too.

I ran my index finger along the name and the number.

Could this mean Cabin Six? Surely there hadn't really been a Cabin Six at one time.

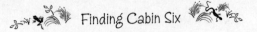

"Hey, check this out, Allie! Someone broke the Ruby Rule!"

Madison pointed out a little artwork in the corner of the new, old piece of wood. It was a carving that had two sets of initials, PG and KC, with a heart in between.

And numbers beside them in parentheses were B6 and G6.

"What do B6 and G6 mean?"

Well, by now, all our cabinmates were crowded around, and that meant they were all breaking the Bliss Rule about not stepping on other people's bedding, since they were all standing on top of my mattress and sleeping bag which was still on the floor.

"Wow! It's a piece of history!" Kayla pushed in to see for herself. "I wonder if PG and KC got married."

"I doubt it," I said. "They had to be just kids when they carved this."

"Hey, Allie," Brooke sat down on my pillow on the floor. "Didn't I see on one of your shows that your grandparents, parents, and even a couple of your aunts and uncles met each other here at Camp 99 Pines?"

I chuckled. "Yeah, that's true."

"So, it could have happened for PG and KC too. That's kind of cool to think about."

Madison repeated her comment, "What do B6 and G6 mean?"

"I'm not sure, but I have an idea," Hayley said. "The same letters and numbers are by these girls' names over here. G2, G3, G4 . . . and they match the signs on the tree at the front of the girls' village. Except there is no G6."

"True," Brooke said. "Unless, of course . . ."

Nobody finished her sentence, because everyone knew the end of her sentence.

Unless, of course, there once was a girls' Cabin Six!

Campfire, Night One

"Allie, do I need a Bible tonight for the campfire?" Madison sat on her top bunk and fumbled around with her flashlight. Dinner had been great—hamburgers, beans, and corn-on-the-cob—and after a game of "Who's Weirder—Camper or Counselor?"—which was just a goofy talent competition, the staff had sent us back up to our villages to prepare for the campfire.

"Because I don't have a Bible, remember? Were you able to bring me one?"

I had heard Madison the first time she asked, but then my mind wandered back to the carvings that were hidden under my mattress. I had to find a way to show my cousins—including Hunter—who wasn't allowed on this side of the camp, what was on that piece of old bench. Not having my phone with the camera was going to make that a tough project.

"Yes, Madison, I brought you one of my Mamaw Kat's Bibles. It was given to her by the founder of this camp, Audrey Gables."

My suitcase sat on a wooden shelf at the end of my bed. I opened it, and rifled through until I found the Bible, wrapped carefully inside one of my towels. Even though Mamaw had said that it needed to get used, I still felt like it was a fragile family heirloom.

"Here it is. It's even a good color, huh? Matches your comforter."

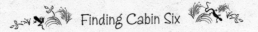

"Thanks." Madison took the Bible from me, but didn't look at it or open it, or cradle it in her arms, or act at all like it was the most important book ever written.

Fine. Give. It. Back.

"I don't want to go tonight." Madison tucked the Bible under her arm and bit her lower lip. "Just being honest."

"Why not? The campfire talks are my favorite. You'll see. It will be inspirational."

Madison shrugged. "Whatever. I guess it *will* be better than sleeping in this creaky cabin tonight. That's going to be a long nine hours."

Okay, I'll give her that. The cabin is creaky, and the nights are long.

Bliss opened the screen door and peeked in.

"Hey, you two, campfire's in ten minutes. We're all sittin' in the same row."

"Madison, why don't you head down with Bliss? I have something to do really quick."

"I'll wait for you."

"I have to go to the bathroom."

"Oh, yuck. I was just there, and it wasn't pleasant." Madison ran for the door. "Bliss! Wait up!"

Then she turned to me. "Don't let Zola catch you walking alone." And then she was gone.

As soon as I was sure she wasn't going to return, I pulled my mattress, with all the bedding, off the wood frame. My pillow slipped onto the floor of the cabin.

"Oh, man. Bliss would freak if she saw that," I said out loud.

Then I pulled my spiral notebook out of my backpack and tore out a few pages. I grabbed my small box of crayons—yes, I like crayons—to do a few "carving rubbings" so I could show my cousins and bring them in on the Cabin Six mystery.

I placed the papers, one by one, over the different carvings,

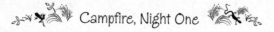

and scribbled away with a brown crayon. It took a couple of tries on the names, since the carvings were shallow. But that one with the heart—that was deep.

PG (B6) ♥ KC (G6)

Who could they be? And was this KC really in Cabin Six?

The bell chimed the five-minute warning. And anyone who's late to campfire loses points for their cabin.

I quickly finished up the rubbings and threw my mattress and bedding back up on the wood frame. Then I tucked the papers in the notebook, stacked my Bible on top, and ran down to the campfire amphitheater.

Madison was saving a seat for me in between her and Ruby.

Okay, I guess that will work. I can help her find verses in the Bible since she's probably not familiar.

I ran to the righthand side of the fourth row of the horseshoe-shaped amphitheater. I climbed over a few girls in my cabin and then squeezed into the skinny spot Madison had saved for me.

"Hey, cousin, I was getting worried about you." Ruby smiled and then scooted over a few inches so I could breathe.

When I finally got situated and looked up I found I was sitting directly across the horseshoe from Nathan Fremont!

He spotted me, and he smiled and waved. His eyes twinkled in the firelight and my cheeks caught on fire again.

Look down, look sideways, look at the stars, but don't look at him! Remember—no love at camp!

"Hey, Madison, do you want me to help you find where today's memory verse is in your Bible?"

She tossed the Bible in my lap. "Of course. This book might as well be written in Greek. I can't find a thing."

I flipped to the New Testament. "Well, some of it was originally in Greek."

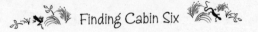

Madison crossed her arms. "Exactly as I thought. Difficult to understand and not applicable to real life."

Huh?

I turned a few more pages, and finally landed on Luke 11:9.

"Here it is. If you can memorize it, we can get more points toward being cabin champs."

Thankfully this was one I already had memorized.

And so I tell you, keep on asking, and you will receive what you ask for.

Keep on seeking, and you will find.

Keep on knocking, and the door will be opened to you.

I showed it to Madison, who didn't seem impressed.

"Ask, seek, knock? What exactly am I asking, seeking, and knocking for? See, this Christian stuff is a just a big mystery to me. And I hate mysteries."

At that moment, Maestro, who had been our camp worship leader for the last three years, walked up to the little stage in front of the campfire amphitheater. He began strumming his guitar, and that sound brought back lots of feel-good memories for me from camps past. I couldn't wait to jump in and sing a chorus or two—it didn't matter what the song was. The tune he began with was new to me, but the words were not.

Sing a new song to the Lord!
Let the whole earth sing to the Lord.
Sing to the Lord, praise his name.
Each day proclaim the good news that he saves.

I recognized those words from Psalm 96—Kendall's favorite verse in the Bible. She has it painted on one of our Scripture boards in the Lickety Split. I glanced over at Kendall, who was sitting with her Cabin Five friends. She was singing at

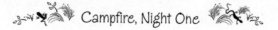

the top of her lungs. Even if I had my eyes closed, I would have known that, because Kendall's beautiful voice rang out louder than everyone's else's. I wished I could be over there sitting next to her.

Jesus is alive in Cabin Five.

But for now, I closed my eyes and tried to harmonize with my cousin.

Great is the Lord. He is most worthy of praise . . .
Let the heavens be glad, and the earth rejoice . . .

The campfire burned hot against my skin, the aroma of pine trees and the sound of chirping crickets filled the air, and my spirit soared. This is what I loved most and waited for all year. An opportunity to worship God, outside, in this beautiful place.

"Allie." I felt a sharp jab in my side. It was Madison's elbow and it jerked me out of my moment.

Grrrr.

"What is it, Madison? I'm trying to worship here."

"I was just wondering something."

The chorus continued.

Give to the Lord the glory he deserves . . .

"What?" I threw my hands in the air. It was out of frustration but the crowd probably thought I was praising.

"If there **had** been a Cabin Six, where do you think it would have been located?"

That was a question that had never entered my mind. Not one time ever, in the many times I had been out here to camp.

"I mean, all those cabins sit up on blocks on a concrete

69

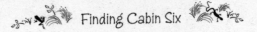

foundation, right? So, if there *had* been a Cabin Six, there should be a slab hidden somewhere. Concrete doesn't just go away that easily."

She was right. My friend Kyra's brother Paul once worked a concrete job during the summer. He was always talking about positioning the rebar and pouring the cement, and the importance of getting it right the first time—because *no one* ever wanted to jack-hammer and start over again. Concrete doesn't go away without a fight.

Tell all the nations "The Lord reigns . . ."

Madison wasn't hearing one single word of the song.

Instead, she grinned and crossed her arms. "I'm going to find it, Allie."

The world stands firm and cannot be shaken . . .

"I'm going to find Cabin Six."

I stood there and my jaw dropped open. Most people would probably think I was singing, but I was trying to figure out this complicated girl next to me.

"So, I guess you don't hate *all* mysteries, then?"

Madison looked right at me, and had the nerve to say, "I like the ones that matter."

CHAPTER 12

Night of Wonders

"Allie." The smooth voice of Nathan Fremont sounded behind me as I gathered my things to head up to the cabin for our nighttime devotions.

The girls in my cabin gave me warning looks with raised eyebrows as I turned to face this cute boy who had crossed over to my side of the horseshoe.

"See you in the cabin in ten minutes, girls," Bliss said. "I'll grab us some snacks from my secret food room stash."

In seconds, my cabinmates were gone, and even though a few kids still hung out in the amphitheater, I felt like I was alone with the boy who once gave me a special bag that began a string of events that proved to me God cared about every single detail of my life.

"So, it's getting dark," Nathan said. "This is a long shot but . . . did you happen to bring my headlamp with you?"

Nathan's headlamp had been one of the objects in the bag he gave me in the airport. It had a desert camo design and the phrase MATT 51415 written on it with permanent marker. Kendall and I figured out that it was a Bible verse—Matthew 5:14–15—that talks about being a light in the world.

Nathan looked down at the ground. "I shouldn't assume anything. You probably don't even have it anymore. It was kind of old and beat-up."

I put my hand out. "Oh, no. I *do* have it! It's just—it's back at the cabin."

Well, actually, it's in my left jeans pocket.

I jammed my hand in to hide the bulge.

Nathan popped his head back up and smiled. "Oh, wow. That's great! Well, I'm sorry you've had to keep it for this long. If you bring it down to the campfire tomorrow, we can exchange lights."

"Exchange?"

"Yeah." Nathan shrugged and I think I noticed a blush. "I got you a new, pretty one."

"You got me a headlamp?"

Nathan laughed nervously. "Yeah. To thank you, for not ditching mine in the trash. At least I hoped you hadn't. My grandma gave me that headlamp, and it's special to me. I felt so dumb for giving you the wrong bag that day at the airport."

I shook my head. "No, it wasn't dumb at all. Some time I'll tell you how God used everything in that bag to teach me some important truths about Him."

"Really? *Everything* in the bag?"

"Yes. He even used the princess Band-Aids! By the way— why *were* you carrying around princess Band-Aids?"

Nathan laughed. "They belonged to my little sister. She's . . . princess-y."

"Oh." I glanced left and right. A few kids lingered so we weren't alone yet. Whew.

But I would love to stay and talk for an hour or so.

"Well, I'm sorry to say that we used all the Band-Aids. It was a bloody trip for me and my cousins. Ha! And that was just on the moving sidewalk in the airport."

"Sounds like an interesting story." Now Nathan was glancing around.

"Well, maybe we'll get a chance to talk about that sometime this week," I said.

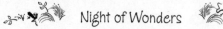

He nodded. "I'd like that." Nathan looked around again, and then pulled something out of his pocket.

"Here. It's dark, so you should have this tonight. I hope you like it."

He handed me a headlamp. It was pink camo, and it had MATT 51415 written by hand on the side of the strap.

"Umm . . . thank you. It's perfect."

Pink camo really is my life.

"Keep moving the beam back and forth in front of you while you walk. To watch out for snakes."

I just stood there and grinned.

"Oh, I guess since you live here you already knew that."

I pressed the little button that switched the beam from white light, to red, to flashing red.

"Well, I better go," Nathan said. "See you tomorrow."

"Okay."

He turned, stepped down some steps to campfire level, and ventured out into the shadows.

"Be careful out there in the . . ."

"Owww!"

"Nathan?"

"I'm okay! Just ran into a tree, that's all!"

I put my hand to my mouth to stifle a laugh. Then I turned, and using both headlamps, I lit up the entire hill that led back to the girls' village.

"We've got popcorn!" Hayley yelled as I entered the cabin. "Bliss is the best!"

Bliss walked around the circle of girls that had formed—all

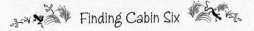

sitting sideways, legs hanging off their bunks—squirting out hand sanitizer.

"Keep the crumbs off the floor or you'll be sweeping in the morning," Bliss said. "Now, what did you girls think about the campfire talk tonight?"

My mind went blank. What *had* they talked about? All I could think about was Nathan and the gift he gave me and wonder when I was going to get to talk to him again.

Ruby was right. Boys are a distraction!

"It's amazing to think that God saw me while I was being formed in my mother's womb . . ." Brooke said.

Ah, yes. Psalm 139. That's what they talked about.

". . . And that God's thoughts about me outnumber the grains of sand. That's a lot of thoughts. How can he be thinking all those thoughts about *me* at the same time he's thinking about everyone else?"

Bliss shook her head, but had a huge smile on her face. "I have no idea. But he's awesome like that."

"It feels kinda weird that God knows everything about me," Julia said. "Even the bad stuff. Makes me want to get rid of the bad stuff."

Bliss smiled and shook her head again. "I know. It's impossible though. We get better, with God's help, but we'll never be perfect. That's why we need Jesus."

There were a few seconds of silence, except for popcorn munches.

Bliss flipped through the pages in her Bible and then looked up at us. "Does anyone have any general questions about God?"

Madison fidgeted on her top bunk. "Yeah, I have a question."

Bliss smiled. "Great! What is it?"

"Well . . ." Madison flipped her hair behind her shoulder

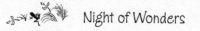

and crossed her arms. "If God is thinking about me *all* the time, and he loves me *so* much, how come he let my parents break up last year? What were his thoughts about me when that was happening?"

Whoa. Tough question on the first night. I hope you have a good answer, Bliss.

Bliss didn't say anything. Instead, she stood up, walked over to Madison's bed, climbed the ladder to her bed and sat down next to her. Then she hugged her.

"I'm so sorry, Madison. I didn't know that about your parents. Can I pray for you?"

She didn't wait for Madison to say yes. She just launched in.

"Dear Lord, thank you for bringing Madison to camp and for putting her in my cabin. She's wondering about a lot of things, Lord. Please help her to understand your love and your ways. Amen."

And that was it. No explanations, no looking up Bible verses, no sharing about how God had helped other girls get through their parents' divorces. Just a prayer that Madison might understand.

"Okay, girls, go brush those teeth and let's get to bed before they blow Taps tonight. We're sure to have an active day tomorrow."

"Is it going to be Survivor Day?" Shelby asked.

Bliss's eyes got big. "No one knows! Not even me. So— sleep is crucial!"

Madison blew her nose. "What's Survivor Day?"

Nobody tell her!

Bliss walked over and put her hand on Madison's shoulder. "My dear, sweet Madison. You are wondering and worrying about a great many things. My recommendation is that you lay your head on your nice, clean pillow, close your eyes, and

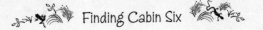

trust that your cabinmates will be here for you no matter what happens this week."

Madison sighed. "Okay, but who has the can of prayer spray?"

Bliss laughed. "Prayer spray?"

"Yeah," Madison said. "To keep away the spiders and the snakes."

Ruby held up a can of Aqua Net. "Right here!" Then she sprayed a little mist in all directions and prayed.

"Lord, keep the spiders and snakes all over in the boys' cabins!"

And Bliss laughed some more.

"I love y'all so much already! This cabin is special, with a capital S!"

CHAPTER 13

A Bunch of Weirdos

If you've ever been to a summer camp, you probably know that all the counselors are a bunch of weirdos. In a good way. And at Camp 99 Pines, the counselors are weirdos for Jesus, which makes for a ton of fun.

During our first recreation session the next morning, after a breakfast of sausage and eggs, we were introduced to all of them.

"Poppy, Panda, Echo, Bliss, and Ember, come on up!" Johan's clothes looked like he'd been sleeping in them for a week straight, but his puffy face looked like he hadn't slept at all.

The five bouncy girl counselors popped up on the box, and as they did, Johan handed them each a pack of different colored stretchy buffs. Those buffs would be worn by every member of their team for the rest of the week. I really wanted to be orange this year, but nothing was going as planned so far, so when Johan handed Poppy—the counselor for girls' Cabin One—the orange buff, I hardly even blinked.

Next came Panda, from Cabin Two. She got the blue.

There went both my favorite colors.

Echo, from Cabin Three, got green. I was okay with not being green, since I have to wear so much green camo on the set of *Carried Away with the Carroways*.

Next up was Bliss, and even before Johan reached in the bag for our color, I knew what it would be.

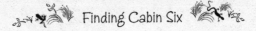

Pink, baby. All. The. Way.

Ember, from Cabin Five, got red. And why not? Red's a power color and everyone knows that Cabin Five rules.

The boys' counselors came up in order next, and they received the colors of the corresponding girls' cabins. Gizmo, orange. Storm, blue. Catfish, green. Cheddar, pink. Buckeye, red, and Blaze, the counselor of boys' Cabin Six—the one with no matching girls' cabin—received the yellow buffs.

The boys from Cabin Six, led by Hunter, immediately broke into a cheer. "When I say 'Yell," you say 'O!'"

"Yell!"

"O!"

"Yell!

"O!"

Johan pointed to the cheering bunch. "Five-million points awarded to Boys' Six for spirit!"

Madison leaned over to me. "I think there's been an information leak. How did they know they were going to get yellow? They couldn't have come up with a cheer that quick."

That made a lot of sense to me. I should have made up a pink cheer last night, because, well . . . pink was taking over my life.

"And Boys' Six doesn't have a partner girls' cabin," Madison said. "So how does that work?"

A great question. And every year, they do it different, so my answer was, "I don't know."

I really hoped that they would just pair Boys' Six with Girls' Four, because, at first glance, Boys' Four was looking like a bunch of saps, and their counselor was named—of all things—Cheddar. As in cheese! And we already knew that Bliss was allergic to cheese.

I did feel sorry that they got the pink buffs, though.

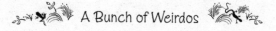

Johan asked the girls' and boys' cabins to bunch up with their new teams, so Cheddar, a guy with yellowy-blonde hair, and his boys ran over. One kid had the buff pulled on his head and over his eyes.

"Hey, look! I have Pinkeye!"

Of course, all the boys laughed at that and not one girl did. Johan yelled into his bullhorn.

"Okay—in two minutes I need a team name from each of you. Make it short and appropriate, and the first team to get their name to me on the box gets a million points."

"And what are we going to do with all these points?" Madison asked. "Can we buy luxuries with them like you see on all the reality shows?"

I started to explain to Madison that there would be an auction at the end of the week where we would use the points to buy needed supplies for the final camp challenge. But before I got two words out, a creepy-stinker from boys' Cabin Four had rushed the box and earned us a million points by giving Johan our "name."

Team Pinkeye.

Seriously, people?

Other, much tougher names streamed in after ours. The orange team became the Solar Flares. The blue team, Hurricane 99. Green, Swamp Rats. Red, Scarlet Fever, and yellow—boys' Cabin Six became the Lightning Rods.

"Okay," Johan yelled into his bullhorn again, "this is how we're going to do it this week. Boys' Six will be rotating teams all week and their point total will be whatever they earn with whatever team they're with. Got it?"

That seemed like a sure win for boys' Cabin Six. After all, whatever team they were with they would be the biggest team.

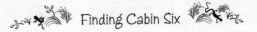

"And for today, Boys' Six Lightning Bolts will be paired with Scarlet Fever!"

Okay, that smarts. Hunter, Parker, Nathan, Kendall, and Lola get to be together? Lord, help me! I'm jealous!

"And today's game is David & Goliath!"

We're doomed.

"I'll see you all out on recreation field two in fifteen minutes. Get your camo on and bathe in bug repellant!"

David and Goliath is your basic Frisbee tag game on steroids. The counselors are the Goliaths and the kids are the Davids. The Goliaths get two red Frisbees each and the Davids get one blue one each. If you're a David and you get hit with a red Frisbee you have to put your blue Frisbee on your head and go to "heaven," which is located on the west sideline of the recreation field.

The Goliaths *always* win, which bugs me since that's not how it is in the Bible.

But this isn't the Bible. This is camp, people! And nothing starts the camp recreation experience out better than getting a nice, fresh bruise from a Frisbee.

"You can stay here in the open," Johan laughed like a villain, "but that would be foolish. You can run in the woods that way . . ." Johan waved his hand toward the east side of the field, ". . . or that way." He pointed south. "And you can go as far as the chain-link fence which marks the end of the camp property. You may NOT go that way . . ." He pointed west. "That way's the swamp, and you do *not* want to meet the beasts that live in the water over there."

I looked at Madison, who had her buff wrapped around her

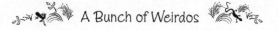

neck with the front part pulled up onto her chin. She appeared to be shivering, maybe with fear.

"When I call, 'Open Field,' those who are still alive must come out onto the field for some head-to-head combat."

I always make it to Open Field. And then I get creamed.

"The last five campers to survive Open Field will earn a million points each for their teams."

Camp 99 Pines always awards points in the millions. We do things almost as big as Texas.

"Any questions?" Johan looked around. Madison shot her hand up in the air.

"Yes, pink girl with the buff over your mouth."

She pulled it down.

"Do head shots count?"

Why is she asking that?

Johan evil-laughed again. "No! If you get pounded in the head, you get to stay in the game. *If* you're conscious."

The whole camp laughed.

Johan pulled an airhorn out of his pocket.

"Okay, when the horn blows, Davids get one minute to get outta here!"

The horn blew. I bolted toward the east woods. But I couldn't run as fast as I normally do, because someone had grabbed the back of my camp shirt and was holding on for dear life.

"Allie, slow down! I can't keep up!" Madison huffed and puffed behind me stretching my shirt out more with every step. Finally, when it was obvious I wasn't going to shake her, I stopped.

"Madison, you don't have to stay with me. You can go wherever you want. Find a bush or a rock, and hide behind it. When you hear the Goliaths go by jump behind a different one."

"But what if we want to attack one of *them*? Isn't it better to have a bunch of us together?"

"Davids *never* attack, Madison."

"Why not? There's way more of us than there are of them."

Hmmm. True.

I tried to explain quickly.

"Because we might lose our team members and we're going for points. So, it's like we're going against the other Davids, too, to see who can survive the longest."

I ran a little bit farther, this time with Madison at my side, to a cluster of bushes that I like to use as my first hideout every year.

I dropped behind a bush and heard the familiar sound of growling and Frisbees being clapped together.

"Get down, Madison," I whispered. "They're coming."

Madison crouched down next to me.

"What if we got a big group together and talked them into ganging up on the Goliaths? We could storm them in a line, all together at first, but then we'll tell Team Pinkeye to retreat at the last minute."

What was she doing? Strategizing?

"Except one person. We should keep at least one out front so that no one suspects that we're setting them up."

She was a devious one—that was for sure.

"It could work," I said. "Let's try it next round. We'll fill everyone in during the break."

Madison smirked. "Why wait till the break? I'll go talk to them in heaven right now."

And with that, she walked out from the bushes, put her Frisbee on her head, and disappeared.

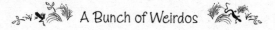

I made it to Open Field, but when I emerged from the woods I spied most of Team Pinkeye in heaven, huddled over by Madison and hanging on her every word. Ruby had survived with me and we found ourselves standing across the center line from Bliss, who was doing some out-of-control winking.

"I think she's planning to protect us so we make the final five," Ruby said.

"Nah," I waved her off with my Frisbee. "The Goliaths never protect *anyone*."

"But Bliss is new. Maybe she doesn't know that."

And sure enough Ruby was right. As soon as Johan blew the airhorn, Bliss ran toward us, backed us into the corner of the field, pretended like she was going to throw the Frisbees, but never let them fly.

We zigged and she zigged. We zagged and she zagged. But not one of us threw a Frisbee.

Bliss winked again, then looked back over her shoulder at the other Goliaths who were taking down Davids left and right.

She finally threw one but way off course. I'm sure it was on purpose. And after just a few minutes into the battle Johan blew the airhorn again.

The only Davids left standing were me, Ruby, Hunter, Nathan, and some tiny, but quick girl named Destiny from the Cabin One Solar Flares.

Score for round one: Lightning Bolts, two million, Team Pinkeye, two million, and Solar Flares, one million.

Bliss ran up to us but didn't high-five. Probably because she didn't have her hand sanitizer. Instead, she just pointed an index finger in our direction.

"I'm all about points for Team Pinkeye. That's my strategy." Then she turned and ran back with her fellow Goliaths.

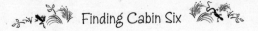

By the time Ruby and I got back over to the sidelines the Davids had unionized.

"We're goin' with Madison's plan," Kendall said. "When the airhorn blows, we're all headin' south. We'll form a line back behind where the old scoreboard blew down, and when we hear the clapping Frisbees we'll charge 'em. It'll be epic! Madison and Boys' Six will be out in front leading the way."

Hunter jumped up and down with excitement. "Goliaths are going down!"

Madison wants to lead the way? And sacrifice herself?

"Okay, Campers! This is the last round since lunch is almost ready. Let's get started!" Johan led us all out to the field and then blew that airhorn long and loud.

All us Davids charged south.

I heard Johan laugh in the bullhorn. "Looks like they're making it easy!" Then he counted to sixty in the speaker—which he never does. And the Goliath Frisbee clapping began.

In the meantime, the Camp 99 Pines middle-school campers formed something even better than a line. It was more like a flying V—like how geese fly. We huddled together, all hundred or so of us—until we heard the stomping and the screaming of wild, weird counselors who enjoy bruising kids with Frisbees.

"Three, two, one . . . charge!" Hunter yelled.

And we charged.

The three kids out front were Hunter, Parker, and Madison. The Madison thing still puzzled me, but whatever. And she was the *first one* hit—with a hard bonk to the forehead! I could have been mistaken, but it looked like she ducked so the Frisbee would hit her there. She then called, "Head shot!" and retreated to the back, where Team Pinkeye was dropping back to meet her.

The war was brutal but swift, and it was gratifying to see

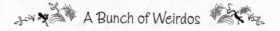

Goliaths with their red Frisbees on their heads, marching to heaven. I'd never seen an assault like this launched *ever* in my summer camp experience. Of course, a lot of Davids went down to defeat too, but Madison was right—there were more of us than there were of them, so in a matter of five minutes, all the Goliaths were in heaven.

And every single member of Team Pinkeye was still alive.

Score: eighteen million points for Team Pinkeye.

And no one suspected a thing.

Madison ran over and gave me a high-five.

"I told you we could do it, Allie."

I smiled. "I've never seen anything like it, Madison."

Madison pointed to her forehead. "Is my goose egg hideous?"

I gently poked the enlarging bump. That thing would be black before the end of lunch.

"It's ghastly," I said. "You're gonna want some ice on that. Let's go see Nurse Tammi."

Madison put her hand out. "Okay, but first I need to go change out of these filthy clothes. I mean, really, why does this place have to be so dirty? I prefer clean wars."

I shook my head, and the bell rang for lunch.

CHAPTER 14

Clues from the Past

"Madi, the hero!" Bliss jumped up from the edge of her bunk, where she was sitting reading the camp schedule. "Way to use your brain to rack us up some big points, and . . . wow—that's a huge bump!"

Bliss came over to Madison and looked at the goose egg more carefully.

"She used her brain *and* her head," I said.

"Hang on a minute." Bliss walked over to her suitcase, lifted the unzipped cover, and pulled a little flashlight out of the netted pouch. She came back and flicked a light in Madison's left eye, and then the right eye.

"Hmmm. Your pupils are working." Bliss smiled. "I've always wanted to do that. How many fingers am I holding up?"

Bliss held up three fingers.

"I don't know," Madison said. "You blinded me with your flashlight." She reached up and grabbed Bliss's hand. "I feel three fingers. Am I right?"

Has Madison always been this funny, or is it her head injury talking?

I laughed. And then I laughed harder when Bliss ran right over to use hand sanitizer.

"Well, you seem okay," Bliss said, "but you better check in with Nurse Tammi. We've got BBs and archery this afternoon so I don't want to take any chances that you'll start shootin' the wrong thing."

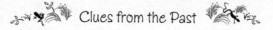

"We'll go see the nurse after we change," I said. "And then we'll head to lunch."

I dug into my suitcase for a change of clothes.

"Hey, Madison, do you need a pair of socks? I brought about eighty pairs."

Madison looked over at me and smiled. "Sure, do you have any in purple?"

I looked through the mass of gray, black, teal, orange, red, tan, green, and yes—pink camo socks. One pair of gray had purple stripes. I held the pair up.

"Are these good?"

Madison came over and snatched them out of my hand. "They're perfect." Then she stared down into my suitcase. "You're not kidding about bringing a lot of socks." She reached in and stirred them around with her hand, which uncovered the plastic bag that Mamaw had given me with the scrapbook in it.

I put my hand on my forehead. "Oh, man! I need to get this to Miss Lindsey!"

Bliss popped her head over our way. "Whatcha got there?"

I pulled out the bag and took out the scrapbook. "These are some pictures of the camp from when my Mamaw came here. Miss Lindsey's collecting them for the 50th year anniversary gala."

"Oooh, can I see?" Bliss reached for the scrapbook, and I placed it in her hands. "Do you know what years these pictures were taken?" She opened the book, and the yellowed plastic pages crackled as she carefully turned them.

"From the looks of them, I would guess a long time ago. Mamaw said she was here as a camper the first year the camp opened. I think she was in high school at the time."

"This is amazing," Bliss said. "I love history."

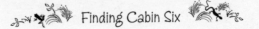

She sat down on my bed (but didn't touch my pillow), and flipped through the pages.

"Looks like the sign at the front entrance hasn't changed."

Madison sat down next to Bliss and leaned in. "Yep, the cabins look the same too. Just as I suspected. No upgrades for fifty years."

Bliss looked up from a picture of a bunch of girls standing in front of a cabin. "Is one of these girls your Mamaw?"

I took a seat on the other side of Bliss and squinted to make out the faces in the black and white photo. It wasn't hard to pick her out, with her dark hair, fair skin, and charming smile.

I pointed. "That's her. Mamaw Kat."

Bliss picked up the book and pulled it closer to her face.

"Your Mamaw's name is Kat? Like in Katherine?"

"Yeah, but no one calls her that anymore."

Bliss dropped the book in her lap. "This is unbelievable! There's my Great Aunt Betsy!" She pointed to a girl standing next to Mamaw Kat. I peered in close—the girl was the spitting image of Bliss.

Madison gasped. "And look what it says right here!" She pointed to some scribbled handwriting in the bottom border of the picture.

High School Girls, Cabin 6

Bliss picked up the book and scrutinized the writing. "That has to be a five that just looks like a six. The girls' village has never had a Cabin Six. Aunt Betsy never mentioned that she was in Cabin Six."

"Sounds like a big cover up if you ask me," Madison said.

"Madison, it's a *Christian* camp. Why would anyone want to cover anything up? That would be deceiving. What would be the goal?"

Madison shrugged. "I don't know, but I just deceived a whole Christian camp for a few million points."

Bliss shook her head. "There has to be a good explanation for this." Then she looked up at me. "Allie, can we keep this scrapbook here until dinner? I want to look at it during afternoon free time."

I shrugged. "Sure. Mamaw just asked me to give it to Lindsey. She didn't say when."

Bliss smiled. "Great. Wow, girls! It looks like we've stumbled onto the mystery of a missing cabin!"

Madison crossed her arms. "I know. And last night, I told Allie I'd find it."

"Want some help?" Bliss wiggled her eyebrows up and down. "Counselors have access to a few more resources . . ."

Now they had me totally sucked in.

"Yes! Let's do it."

"Oh, and you know what else we should do?" Madison had her sneaky, goose egg, game face on.

"What?" Bliss's eyes got wide.

"Let's take the dinger out of the bell!"

Madison sat on the cot in Nurse Tammi's office with an icepack on her forehead.

"There's a kid with hives I have to go track down," Nurse Tammi said. "You're looking good, sweetie. You're free to go if you want. Keep the icepack."

She walked out the screen door toward the mess hall.

"Madison—I can't believe you told Bliss about the dinger."

Madison lowered her icepack. "Why? She's just like us—I can see the rascal in her. And I know she wants us to win cabin champs."

"But counselors aren't usually involved in big plans like that, since it involves sneaking around at night."

Madison leaned forward. "Do you think I'm gonna be wandering around at night knowing Zola Simms is out there, without an adult by my side? NO. This is *much* safer."

"Madison, the Zola Simms story isn't true."

Madison stood up and brushed herself off. "And until today you didn't think that Cabin Six ever existed either. So maybe it *did* burn down, and maybe Zola *is* waiting to snatch the last camper. What do you think of that?"

I shook my head. "I still say that there's a reasonable explanation for the disappearance of that cabin."

"And we're also going to be *reasonable* by involving our counselor in the disappearance of the bell dinger. Hey—let's do it tonight! Early in the week—Johan won't be expecting it. I bet he's still reeling from losing at David and Goliath."

Who is this girl? It's like she went from being a whiny, scaredy-cat to being camp director.

I sighed. "I think you've sprained your brain. Let's go have lunch."

We had barely stepped out of the nurse's hut, when we were met by two groups of people coming from separate directions.

One group was made up of three grownups. Two older men, both wearing dark suits, and a blonde woman wearing a butter-colored suit, who I knew. Her name was Ellen and she worked for Best Bayou Realty. She was the agent who sold our house to the Doonsberrys back in November.

"Allie Carroway! It's so great to see you!" Ellen came over to shake my hand. "I hear your new house is almost ready. I'm so happy for you!"

I tried to put on a smile. "Thank you, ma'am."

One of the guys—the older, pudgy one with the receding hairline and little round glasses—scowled. "Ellen, come along. We're not to bother the campers."

Ellen looked over at him and put on a serious face. "Of course, Mr. Gables. I'm very sorry."

Ellen grinned at me and waved a little but then scooted back over with the serious gentlemen.

Mr. Gables? Could that be Patterson Gables?

The trio turned away from me and as they did the other group, made up of boys from Cabin Six, came flying from the other direction.

"Blaze killed a snake!" Hunter yelled. "We gotta find Hawk!"

Hawk is the camp dean. He's in charge of serious things. Like snake sightings and kills, and well . . . snake sightings and kills. That's all I've ever seen Hawk really taking care of. Hawk's speech to campers the first night is always the same:

Stay away from snakes. Do NOT try to kill them. Report all sightings to me, and DO NOT swim in the lake or in any water on camp grounds except the pool.

And the tradition is, whenever a *counselor* kills a snake, they have to skin it and mount it on the wall in the counselor's resource room. I've been in there a few times with my dad and it's quite a slithery collection.

Nathan was in the group of boys who came running, looking for Hawk. So was Parker.

"What kind of snake was it?" I asked.

Hunter huffed and puffed. "Blaze thinks it's a coral snake."

"Is that poisonous?" Nathan asked. When he did his dimples sank in on both sides of his cheeks.

"Yes," I answered. "But at least it wasn't a copperhead. I hate copperheads."

"Hey—there's Hawk over there." Parker pointed to the path

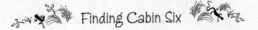

that leads to Bluff Springs Lake, where campers can go boating during free time.

"Hawk!" Hunter yelled. "We got ourselves a dead snake over here!"

Hawk, who looks huge even from a distance, carried a hatchet and began a fast jog toward us.

Madison put her fingers up to her goose egg.

"Can we go, Allie? I don't want to be present when the . . . dead reptile arrives."

"Sure, let's go see if there's any lunch left."

Madison and I scurried off, even though I kind of wanted to talk to Nathan about snakes . . . and pretty much anything else.

"Hey, Allie! Come sit with us!" Kendall yelled from her table, where only she and Lola remained from Cabin Five. Ruby was sitting with them too.

I stood there, between Madison and my cousins, trying to figure out what to do.

"Allie," Madison said, "go sit with them. I'll be fine over here with Shelby and Brooke."

"Are you sure?"

"Yeah. You've been looking out for me all morning. And except for the concussion, I'm fine . . . fine . . . fine . . . fine . . ."

As she said that, she jerked her head back and forth, like she was a robot, stuck in a program.

I cracked up.

Madison then took her hand and slapped her cheek, which stopped the "fines."

Then she laughed. "I'll see you later, at archery."

Who is this girl? She's acting normal. And she's funny.

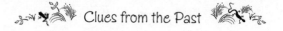

And yet, I still couldn't trust that she had entirely good motives for sending me over to the cousins. Too much stuff from the past. Building trust takes time.

I picked up my pace and placed my tray down in between Lola and Kendall.

"How's the princess cabin?" Kendall asked. "That was quite a victory at David and Goliath. I think y'all set us up."

I smiled. "I'll never tell."

Lola wiped some spaghetti sauce from her mouth with a napkin.

"Allie, have you seen that grumpy old guy walking around with those other two people? Everyone says that's Patterson Gables. I can't believe he would have the nerve to come around when campers are here. Doesn't he care that our hearts are breaking?"

"I think that other guy with him is the buyer," Kendall said. "At least that's what Parker said."

"And that lady in the butter-colored suit is the realtor who sold our house," I added. "So yes, Parker's probably right."

Ruby twisted her fork around in her noodles. "What are we gonna do, Allie?"

I shrugged. "I'm fresh out of ideas." I glanced over at the Cabin Four table, where Madison was showing off her goose egg to Shelby and Brooke. "But you know what, I bet Madison would have some suggestions if we asked her."

"Madison?"

'Yeah. I mean she has a devious streak to her. She already outsmarted all of you *and* the counselors at David and Goliath, and now she's making plans to take the dinger out of the bell . . ."

I immediately covered my mouth.

Oops. I shouldn't have said that to rival cabin members.

"The dinger? She's gonna steal the dinger?" Kendall smiled. "I want in! When's it happenin'?"

I had to think about that for a minute. Had any cabins in the history of Camp 99 Pines worked *together* to remove the dinger?

I guess there was always a first time for everything. It was shaping up to be that kind of week.

"I can be the climber," Ruby said as she slopped some noodles into her mouth.

"I'll take care of photography," Lola said. "We'll want to record this for posterity."

"We need to bring Hunter too," Kendall said. "He'd be so disappointed if we all did this without him."

"Wait." I put out a hand. "We're getting boys involved now too?"

"Why not? I'll tell Parker and you can invite Nathan. G4, G5, and B6—stealing the dinger. It'll be an epic way to celebrate our last year at Camp 99 Pines."

That comment by Kendall sort of sent my emotions on a roller coaster.

Last year at camp? Invite Nathan? And what about Madison? And don't forget that Bliss knows what we're planning.

"Madison wants to do it tonight," I said. "Because Johan won't be expecting a prank so early in the week."

"That's brilliant!" Lola beamed.

"I got it, y'all." Kendall took out a pen and started drawing on a napkin. Everyone leaned in to see. "We'll pretend we're going on a potty run, and we'll meet in front of the guest lodge near the girls' village at midnight. Then we'll make our way to the bell where we'll ask the boys to meet us at 12:05. Then, we form a human pyramid, and Ruby can climb up and get the dinger. That way we won't waste time draggin' a ladder around.

We'll hide the dinger and get back to the cabins before our counselors even start to worry."

"Oh, we won't be worried."

The young woman's scratchy voice behind our huddle startled us. Forks dropped, spaghetti sauce splattered, and we all turned to see Bliss *and* Ember—the counselor for girls' Cabin Five—standing there, crossing their arms.

Bliss smiled. "Like Ember said, we won't be worried, because we're goin' with y'all."

CHAPTER 15

Bullseyes

I always say I'm going to practice my archery and shooting skills more during the year so I have a chance to win the girls' sharpshooter and archer awards at camp.

But I don't, so I never do.

I really love it though—especially archery. But my arrows always fly a little higher than I'd like.

"Bullseye!" Ruby yelled, after she let her arrow fly.

Ruby always gets bullseyes.

Turns out the girls in Cabin Four were pretty good archers. Even Madison managed to get a couple of arrows close to the middle right off the bat and this was the first time she'd ever held a bow.

"I just imagine that if I hit that ring I can instantly be transported to my comfy bedroom with my clean, cushy rug and snuggly puppy."

She pulled back the bowstring, aimed, and let the arrow fly.

And sure enough that arrow landed right in the middle of the circle.

"Bullseye!" she yelled.

You should try Madison's trick, Allie! Use your imagination. What do you want more than anything right now? Take aim, and go for it!

There were a lot of things to choose from but the one that seemed to rise to the top was this:

I just want to have a fun week at camp! No drama, no complications, just smooth, easy, fun. After all, it may be my last.

"Okay, here goes nothin'."

I pulled back, took aim, and let it fly.

I must have had a muscle spasm or something, because the arrow flew over the top of the target and hit a tree.

"Well, at least you hit somethin'," Bliss said.

I took the bow down from my shoulder and examined it.

"I've never totally missed the target." I grabbed another arrow out of the basket and tried again.

Fun week, calm week, victorious week. That's what I want.

I pulled back. The arrow flew and hit Julia's target next to mine.

"Thanks for the points, Allie," Julia laughed.

What in the world was going on here? This was just a silly technique to rack up archery points.

Or maybe it's a little more than that.

That small voice inside was one I'd heard before but it always takes me by surprise, showing up when I least expect it. And this was a silly time—when I was holding a bow and arrow.

I set the bow down so I could watch my new friends in Cabin Four take their turns. They were nailing the bullseyes left and right.

I *didn't want to be with these girls, God. In fact, I prayed for something else.*

Madison pulled back again and right before she let the arrow go, she said, "If I get a bullseye, it's a spa day followed by chicken alfredo for dinner and raspberry cheesecake for dessert."

Of course, she hit the bullseye.

"Yes!" she yelled.

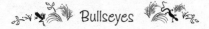

Bliss laughed. "Well, Chef Gumbo told me it's gonna be sloppy joes tonight, but keep that imagination going, girl. Our cabin's way out in the lead with the archery points."

I tried again and another of my arrows went in the wrong direction.

"Well, you're sure not getting whatever you're wishing for," Madison said.

You have no idea.

I squinted at Madison. "Don't get cocky, Miss Beginner's Luck."

Madison looked over and examined me. "I think you're just trying too hard because you're Miss Experienced Camp Girl. Relax and go with the flow."

Go with the flow. Stop trying to control your week.

I shook my head around, trying to dislodge that last thought. But I couldn't because it wasn't mine. It was God again. How do I know? Because I would *never* tell myself to stop controlling things. If I did, things could get crazy.

I specialize in that. In a good way.

"Whatever!" I said, a little too loud.

Oops.

"Someone's a little grumpy," Madison said, and she let another arrow fly into the bullseye. "But I guess maybe I have enough points to cover you." Madison looked over and winked, and our archery leader, Pepper, called for us to put down our bows and retrieve our arrows.

"Allie Carroway, there's a step stool behind the targets you can use to get that one out of the tree."

BBs were next, and I was much better at that. Probably because

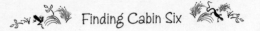

we do a little shooting while filming *Carried Away with the Carroways*.

And the best part of BBs was that Madison had to kiss the gun because she released the safety too soon.

"Next time you have to lick it," our BB instructor, Domino, said.

Bliss couldn't watch. "I'll meet y'all down by that log when your turn is over."

During the break, while Cabin Three took their turns shooting, I had a chance to discuss "Operation Dinger" with Bliss and the rest of the cabinmates.

"You mentioned this to your cousins?" Madison put a hand on her hip.

"I'm sorry, it just slipped out."

Madison pushed her hand into her now out-of-control red mop.

"And you want to involve the boys too?" Bliss put a fist to her chin. "This doesn't have anything to do with *love*, does it?"

I laughed nervously. "Well, yeah, but it's love for my cousin, Hunter. Ever since he was adopted we've made it a priority to include him in everything."

Bliss stared into my eyes. I hoped she didn't see any clues of a crush on a certain California surfer.

"Okay," she said. "We'll do it. Girl's Four and Five, and Boy's Six. But we can't take everyone. We'll sound like a stampede of cattle running through the camp. We'll wake Johan, and if he catches us, we're toast, and Ember, Blaze, and I will be thrown in the swamp as an Allibeaver snack."

It's tradition at Camp 99 Pines that any counselors caught aiding campers in a prank during the week be thrown in the swamp on the last day of camp—while everyone in the camp cheers. The "Allibeaver" is a fictional character—a monster

that is half-alligator and half-beaver—made up to scare the little kids from jumping into the lake to try to swim during their boating activities.

"But we need lots of people to make the pyramid tall enough for me to reach into the bell," Ruby said.

Bliss nodded. "I think we can do it with ten."

And so we decided on the ten: me, Madison, Ruby, Kendall, Lola, Hunter, Parker, Nathan, Bliss, and Blaze—the Boys' Six cabin counselor.

"Ember can keep an eye out while we're gone, which won't be long," Bliss said. "Let's talk to the rest of the girls during free time and I'll clue Blaze in at dinner."

"Where should we hide the dinger?" Ruby asked.

Madison put an index finger to the side of her face.

"I think we should put it at the bottom of the pool."

CHAPTER 16

Nappy-Time?

After our rec time, and before free time, we always have what is called "Nappy-Time." It's a thirty-minute quiet time when we all have to be in our cabins "sleeping." Usually the only person sleeping is the counselor and the rest of us are eating candy under the covers and making plans for what we're going to do during free time.

But on Monday afternoon in Cabin Four, the one who was most awake was Bliss.

And she was studying through the crackly pages of Mamaw's scrapbook.

"Girls, check this out! Guess who was the winner of the sharpshooter award the first year? My aunt Betsy!"

A few of us came out from our candy-filled sleeping bags to take a peek at the scrapbook.

"I bet she didn't have to kiss a gun," Madison said. "I can still taste it. Does anyone have a really strong mint?"

Hayley handed her one and Madison popped it in her mouth, which started her on a tear of powerful sneezing.

"That's good," Bliss said. "Just sneeze out that door, please. You're purging all the gun germs from your system. Here, girls, have some hand sanitizer."

Bliss took out a brand-new gallon-sized container from her suitcase and we had squirts all around.

"So, did you find any more clues about the disappearance of Cabin Six?" I asked.

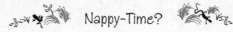

Bliss shook her head. "No, but I thought *this* was interesting." She pointed to a flyer that advertised a fundraising dinner and silent auction for supporters of the camp.

"It says right here, 'For future generations—keep Camp 99 Pines open for another season. We're relying on our faith and on your generosity.'"

And then it specified a date for the dinner. The end of August. And there was a picture of a middle-aged couple with a teenaged-boy standing in between them. Below the picture it said, "Quincy, Audrey, and Patterson Gables."

And at the bottom of the flyer, it said,

"Till all the lost are found."

"What does that mean?" Madison asked.

"It comes from a story Jesus told about a shepherd who loved each of his sheep so much that he left 99 of them alone so he could go and search for one that was lost," Bliss said. And then she looked up into Madison's eyes. "The story shows how much God cares about each one of us. He'll go anywhere, do anything, and risk everything to find you, Miss Madison. Do you know that?" Bliss smiled.

Whoa, a serious spiritual moment during Nappy-Time! We all waited for Madison's response.

She stepped back from our little huddle. "Hmmm. Well, I'm not sure he cares *that* much. But I would still love for him to come rescue me out of *this* swamp."

Yes, Jesus. Please come get Madison out of her swamp.

CHAPTER 17

Campfire Talk #2

The plan was set—and it was a good one. I couldn't imagine a better crew for this epic prank. We decided to leave a note in the bell, so when Johan went to ring it in the morning, and he heard no clang, he would climb up and find this little message:

```
I heard the bell on Christmas Day,
But not today, but not today.
And that's because we got you good.
The dinger's gone in the morning!
            Signed, Sneaky Campers
                . . . heeheehee!
```

Kendall wrote the poem, and of course it was a song, sung to the tune of the Christmas carol, "I Saw Three Ships."

"How are we going to stick the note on the bell?" Madison leaned over me to whisper to Bliss during our night two campfire talk.

"Hunter always carries duct tape with him," I said.

"And we get points if Johan doesn't figure out who took it till Friday, right?" Madison was scribbling something on a notepad that she had tucked into Mamaw's lavender Bible.

"That's my understanding," Bliss said. "If he can't come up with evidence that reveals we took it we'll get fifty-million extra points."

"And what happens if we get caught?" Madison asked.

"Then we get an S.O.S.," I said.

"S.O.S?"

"Special Opportunity to Serve," Ruby said. "Like picking up all the broken water balloons from the field after water day or scrubbing the bathhouse . . ."

"Oh, no. Then we WON'T be getting caught," Madison said.

"I agree," Bliss slapped her knee. "There isn't enough hand sanitizer in the entire world for that."

Maestro jumped up on stage and began strumming some of our most favorite worship songs. Again, joy filled my heart and I thanked the Lord for Camp 99 Pines.

But Madison scribbled away on her notepad the whole time.

Finally, when I was totally distracted by her rudeness and wanted to pick her up and send her crowd-surfing down to the bottom of the amphitheater our camp speaker, Pastor Bo, got up and asked a question:

"How many of you haven't taken a shower yet at camp?"

Hands shot up proudly from the boys' side of the amphi-theater. I searched for Nathan, but couldn't find him. That was good for now. Ha! He was probably in the shower.

Most of the girls' hands stayed down. I *knew* most of them had taken showers. The line tonight had been ultra-long. One girl was in there so long that she finally got yelled at.

"At home I take hour-long showers," she argued from the other side of the curtain.

To which, my cousin Kendall, who was next in line replied, "THIS IS NOT YOUR HOME!"

Pastor Bo pinched his nose between his thumb and index finger. "I thought something smelled funny on this side of the camp."

"We smell like the woods!" Hunter said.

That's nothing to brag about, cousin.

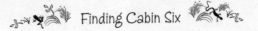

The boys hooted and hollered and the girls groaned.

Pastor Bo looked over at the girls. "Well, you just wait, girls, you're going to be dirty again tomorrow, and the next day, and the next day, and you'll have to take that shower again, and again, and again . . ."

Madison crossed her arms. "And what horrible dirt games are we going to play tomorrow and the next day and the next day?"

I laughed a little to myself.

Pastor Bo continued. "And just think about *this*—that's just your outside getting dirty. What about all the dirt on the inside? The dirt in your heart? That takes more than a simple shower to clean up."

Madison uncrossed her arms, looked over at me briefly, and dropped her chin.

"The Apostle Paul, who was a follower of Jesus, wrote this in a letter to the church in Rome:

> No one is righteous—not even one.
> No one is truly wise,
> No one is seeking God.
> All have turned away;
> All have become useless.
> No one does good,
> Not a single one.

Madison scribbled a note on her pad and handed it to me.
NO ONE?
I took my pen and scribbled under it.
YEP.
Then, Pastor Bo went on to tell a story about when he was

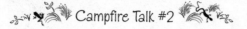

in fourth grade and he decided he was tired of doing his math homework. Each day he tore out the page from the workbook, shoved it way back in his desk, and told his mom that he finished his work in class and didn't have homework.

"It worked for a few weeks, or so I thought," Bo said. "But then, guess what happened? It was time for my parent/teacher conference, and I was invited to come along. And during that conference, my teacher told me that she hadn't received any math work from me in a long time. I acted surprised and assured her I had been turning it in. She didn't come right out and accuse me of lying, but she did ask if maybe instead of turning it in I had left it in my desk instead. 'May I take a look?' she asked."

A collective groan sounded from the whole kids' camp.

"Yeah, so you know what happened next, right? She starts pulling out all my papers! They were smashed and some were folded up all accordion-like since they were stuffed back there so tight for so long."

"Busted!" some boy yelled from the crowd.

Pastor Bo frowned. "Yeah, I was caught. And then came the consequences. For six weeks, I had to go straight home from school, do my homework for the day, and then I had to work on all my past-due math pages. I even had to stay home on the weekends! No friend time, no TV, no parties, nothing. Not until I paid for my wrongdoing and got those math pages caught up. It was the longest six weeks of my life!"

"You shouldn't have done it," some girl yelled out.

Pastor Bo laughed. "You're right. I was sure a fool to think I could hide all that and no one would find out. But I learned my lesson, and thankfully, I could make it all up and get back on the right track. And I didn't end up flunking fourth grade math either."

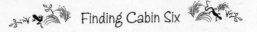

"Good job, Bo!" That was Hunter again.

"But, friends, the dirt in our hearts that God calls sin has a much bigger consequence than I suffered when I hid my fourth-grade math papers. The Bible says that this sin separates us from God because God is Holy and he can't be in the presence of sin."

Madison's chin sank even lower now. She was staring at her feet.

Pastor Bo asked us to look up Romans 3:23 in our Bibles and asked someone to read it out loud.

Parker offered.

"For everyone has sinned. We all fall short of God's glorious standard."

Madison glanced up for a moment to look at Parker, and I watched as their eyes met.

"So, who does it say sins?" Bo asked.

"Everyone," Parker repeated.

Madison straightened back up and I watched as she scanned the crowd.

What's going on in her head, God? But more importantly, what's going on in her heart?

My heart was pounding at that moment, remembering the time a few years ago at camp when I felt God telling me that I needed to deal with my sin. Is this what Madison was feeling right now?

She's lost, God. Leave the 99 and go get her!

Pastor Bo turned a page in his Bible. "Yes, boys and girls, sin is a terrible thing. And it has a much worse consequence than six weeks of long division."

Bo then asked for a girl to read Romans 6:23. Ruby offered this time.

"The wages of sin is death . . ."

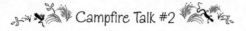

Bo held out his hand. "Stop there. Death! Let's think about that. How many of you want to die?"

No one raised their hands. And the whole camp was quiet.

"You mean there isn't a person here who wants to pay the consequence for their sin?"

"I'd rather do math," a boy said.

Pastor Bo smiled. "I agree. I don't want to die either. But I know someone who *did* want to die. For me, for you, for everyone who ever lived in the past, and for everyone who will ever live in the future. And that's God's son, Jesus. He willingly paid the penalty for our sin so we could have a chance to live forever as God's children."

Still dead silent.

Pastor Bo pointed to Ruby. "Okay, my friend, you may read the whole verse now."

Ruby cleared her throat and read loudly and proudly.

"For the wages of sin is death, but the free gift of God is eternal life through Christ Jesus, our Lord."

"Whew, that's a relief," another boy said.

"Yes, it is." Bo smiled. "For those of us who ask for forgiveness and choose to receive that gift, we are forgiven. When God looks at our hearts, he no longer sees the sin. He just sees Jesus. And in case you were wondering, after Jesus died, he didn't stay dead. He rose from the grave three days later—proving that he has power over everything—sin, death, sickness, sadness, hopelessness, fear, and every bad thing that happens in this broken world that we now call home."

Madison was scribbling again on her notepad. When she noticed me looking over her shoulder, she held it up so I could see the big word she wrote:

DIVORCE.

I nodded.

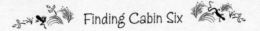

"He promises to make all things new." Pastor Bo just sat there, looking out at the crowd.

Maestro began strumming on his guitar and Bo told us that he was going to talk more about the "new" part tomorrow night. Then he prayed and he challenged us to go back to our cabins and talk about how we had personally been affected by sin in our world, and if we were brave, to talk about the sin in our own lives that separates us from God.

He asked us to leave quietly, and to not talk with anyone until we returned to our cabins.

While we were walking away from the amphitheater, Bliss pulled me aside.

"I'm going to go talk to Blaze for a minute. When you get back to the cabin, tell the girls that I just want them to lay on their beds and write down their thoughts about all they heard tonight. No talking. When I get back, we'll pray."

I nodded. "Got it."

And that's what we did. Everyone snuggled into their sleeping bags. You could hear the scribbling.

And from Madison's bunk, I heard a little sniffling too—and lots of writing and page turning. I kept sneaking a look up there. She must have filled up ten pages in her journal.

CHAPTER 18

Operation Dinger

It was 11:55 p.m., and I was scared out of my wits.

And I had a little dilemma.

Which headlamp should I take with me?

I wanted to take Nathan's—the brown one. But if he saw me with it, would he ask for it back? I wasn't ready to give it up.

I brought both.

"Are we ready, girls?" Bliss—who had her face covered with camo paint, and her hair all tucked in a dark green beanie—gathered our whole cabin of girls together in a huddle. She squirted our hands with sanitizer.

"This little operation could get me eaten by the Allibeaver at the end of the week so I want you to know, just in case this is my last week on earth, that I couldn't have asked for a better group of girls to be in my cabin. And I hope to see y'all in heaven."

We all giggled just a bit. And then we put our hands out for a quiet cheer.

"Princesses in camo, on three," Bliss whispered.

We pumped our stacked hands three times, up and down.

"Princesses in camo!" we gave our most enthusiastic whisper-yell.

Then Ruby, Madison, Bliss, and I exited our sparkly pink princess cabin, and entered the dark, shadowy, swampy night, tiptoeing our way to pick up Lola and Kendall at the girls' lodge.

Two bushes moved as we approached the lodge and it made me jump about a mile.

"Gotcha!" Kendall said. "How do you like our camo?"

Kendall and Lola giggled and I shushed them.

"If you keep that up we'll get caught and Bliss will be Allibeaver dessert."

Lola snapped a picture and the flash from her camera blinded me.

"This is not starting off well," I said.

"Madison, you look tough!" Kendall reached over and punched a camo-clad and painted up Madison in the arm.

She smiled. "Thanks. I'm ready for action."

"Good," Bliss said. "You're all here. Let's go meet the boys. NO more talking from here on out. Remember—Johan sleeps outside in a hammock."

Oh, yeah. The old hammock trick. Luckily it was near the entrance to the boys' village.

At exactly 12:05, we approached the bell. But no boys were in sight.

We stood there for another five minutes—with no lights and in the pitch black, no-moon night.

I reached out to get Bliss's attention. "Should we just do it ourselves?"

Bliss flicked her flashlight up toward the inside of the bell.

"No, we need everyone to lift Ruby up there."

A shiver went up my neck and tingled my head. We waited five more minutes.

And then, with absolutely no warning, Nathan Fremont was standing right next to me.

"Hi, Allie. Sorry we're late," he whispered.

I almost screamed. In fact, I opened my mouth to scream, but Hunter put his gloved hand over my mouth just in time.

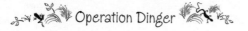

"We had to crawl past Johan—one by one," Blaze said. "That guy moves a lot in that hammock. But these guys made less noise than a lizard."

Bliss sighed. "Okay, let's move it. Do we have the note and the tape?"

Kendall held up a paper. Hunter produced the tape.

"I'll take those," Ruby said, and she strapped a headlamp on to her head.

"Boys," Blaze whispered. "We've got the bottom."

Blaze, Parker, Nathan, and Hunter dropped to the ground in a crawl position to become the bottom row of our pyramid. Then Kendall, Lola, and Madison hopped up, forming the second level. Bliss—the gymnast—and I—the flyer on my cheer squad—took the third level.

"Okay, I'm climbing up," Ruby whispered and she began to ascend the human ladder. When she got to the top she stepped on Bliss's back so she could stand up and reach into the bell.

But she didn't come right down with the dinger.

"Ruby, what's going on?" I asked.

She crawled back down. "My arms are too short. I need about twelve more inches."

My cheerleading instinct popped in. "What if Bliss and I stand and clasp hands and you stand on that?"

Ruby shook her head. "I don't think I have the balance."

"You can do it, Allie," Nathan said. "I've seen you on the show. You're a killer gymnast." Then he gave me a thumbs-up.

And who can say no to that?

So, we formed the pyramid again. Same guys on the bottom, but Ruby changed places with Lola so she could help Bliss lift me up. She's got strong arms and legs from all her volleyball playing.

I looped the duct tape around my wrist, put the note in my

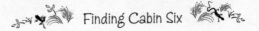

teeth, and pulled out a headlamp from my pocket to strap on my head. It was the brown one.

Oh, well.

I shrugged and began to climb. Lola and Bliss formed the perfect team, lifting me up a little too fast. I almost clanged the bell with my head.

"A little lower," I said.

I was all-in now. If Johan woke up and found us, he's probably pick us all off with a paint-ball gun.

Don't get distracted, Allie. Just get the dinger.

First, I taped the note to the inside of the bell. Then I reached up with my hand, and tried to unhook the dinger. It was in there tight and it took me a minute, since I had to make sure I didn't hit the side of the bell with it which could send the entire camp running out of their villages for breakfast.

Finally, after a little wiggling and turning, it came loose and Lola and Bliss lowered me down.

"Got it," I whispered. I flicked off my headlamp and climbed down.

"Okay, let's go throw it in the pool," Madison said, while brushing herself off.

And as we took off down the road to the pool house, we heard a voice yell, "I CAN'T SEE YA, BUT I'M GONNA GET YA!"

Johan.

"Scatter!" Blaze said. "Stay with a buddy and get back to the cabins any way you can."

My pulse raced, and I grabbed the person closest to me. Madison.

She looked over—terror in her eyes.

"Stay with me," I said. "We're NOT getting caught."

Bodies ran in all directions and I headed back toward the girls' village, but not on the dirt path. I pulled Madison through

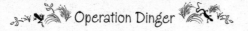

the woods on the side of the path while ducking and weaving between the pine trees. I heard footsteps, running, echoing through the camp.

We had made it to the entrance of the girls' village. About a hundred yards from the lodge—where female guests of the camp stay.

"Let's get over there. Maybe the doors are open."

We waited until things were quiet and then darted to the lodge, flew up the steps, checked the door.

Locked.

A flashlight beam shone in the distance. Who knew if it was friendly light or enemy light?

I grabbed Madison. "Quick, we're goin' under."

"Under the lodge? I'll die."

I pulled her by her clothes down the steps and behind the lodge. Then I got down on all fours and crawled under a corner, feet first, into the space between the lodge floor and the concrete foundation. It was a squeeze but I managed to get all the way in and pull Madison in next to me.

I was glad to have my arms and legs covered by clothes and my hair wrapped up in a beanie. Spiders, you know.

It took a minute or two for us to get settled, laying there on our stomachs, peering out at the darkness. I heard Madison breathing a little hard and was surprised that I—the asthma kid—wasn't. And it was a good thing because I realized that in all the excitement of getting ready for "Operation Dinger," I had forgotten to strap on my wrist pack.

"How long do we need to stay here?" Madison whispered.

"Until we're sure Johan is gone."

"Can snakes bite through your clothes?"

"Let's not think about that right now, shall we?"

"Do you still have the dinger?"

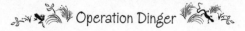

"Yeah."

"Good."

We waited. Ten minutes. Twenty minutes. I kept hearing noises, which could have been lizards darting around in the leaves, but we couldn't take that chance so we didn't move. Finally, after what seemed like an hour, I flicked on my light.

"Madison, I think the coast is clear . . . Madison?"

Her breathing had settled down a while ago. She was asleep!

"Huh?" She yawned. "Where are we? Oh, yeah, the snake den." She lifted her head a few inches and looked around. "Am I dead?"

I giggled. "Not yet. I think we can go now."

I flashed my light around again just to make sure. Then I strapped it to my head so I could use my hands to crawl out of our hiding place. As I was strapping it on, Madison grabbed me by the arm.

"Allie! Look!"

My heart started pounding, and I turned my head in the direction Madison was pointing. My light shined on the corner of the concrete where something had been carved into it.

G6.

"This is it," Madison said. "This is the place where girls' Cabin Six used to be—before it disappeared, or burned down, or whatever happened to it."

I flashed my light a little closer. Sure enough, it said G6 and it had a circle drawn around it. Probably carved into the concrete when it was poured, before it dried.

Madison smirked. "I told you I'd find it."

117

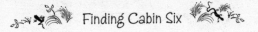

It took Madison and me another hour to make it back to Cabin Four. First, we had to climb the fence at the pool, and plop that silly dinger in.

"We should get a hundred million points for that," Madison said. "That was the scariest thing I've ever done."

"Yeah." I smiled. "I don't think I'd try it again, that's for sure."

"What time is it?"

I checked my sports watch.

"One-thirty."

"Do you think we have time to go check under the other cabins to see if they have numbers engraved on the concrete?"

I shrugged. "It's on the way back. Let's be quick about it."

So we climbed back over the fence and crept down the path from the pool. The camp was dead silent now. We passed by the girls' lodge on our way into the entrance of the village.

Wow, God. Of all the hiding places I could have chosen!

We checked cabins one, two, and three. Sure enough, they all had G1, G2, and G3, carved into the concrete, right on the corner of their foundations. And we also noticed that all the cabins had a matching mark carved on the bottom left corner of the back wall.

"I think that's enough proof," I said, and we both ducked into the bathroom to make a pit stop before returning home.

"Oh, thank the Lord!" Bliss was at the sink, washing camo paint off her face. She ran over—with her wet hands—to hug us. "I've been searching for you girls everywhere." She wouldn't let go. "I didn't care if Johan found me or if I got thrown into the swamp, I just prayed, Lord, help me find my two little lost sheep."

Then she pulled away and gave us a once-over. "Are y'all okay?"

"Oh, yes," Madison said. "We're better than okay. We just found the foundation of Cabin Six."

CHAPTER 19

Survivor Day

An airhorn pierced the early morning quiet. That was followed by the voice of Johan on the bullhorn.

"Wake up, campers, and get to the box in fifteen minutes. Oh, yes—it's SURVIVOR DAY!"

"Oh, Lord, let this be a dream," Bliss said.

I turned in my sleeping bag, lifted my head, and my dark-blonde tangles covered my eyes.

"Survivor Day? On a Tuesday?"

Johan continued on the bullhorn. "Yes, on a TUESDAY! HAHAHAHAHA . . ."

Next came a thud. Ruby had rolled off her bunk onto the cushy princess rug.

"Owww."

Good thing she was totally inside her fluffy sleeping bag.

"PREPARE FOR MUD! LOTS OF IT!" More laughing from the bullhorn.

"Somebody go shove him back in his hammock." Bliss wiggled out of her sleeping bag and starting flinging clothes out of her suitcase.

The girls in Cabin Four emerged from their sleeping bag cocoons, one-by-one, all stretching, yawning, and full of questions about last night's shenanigans.

"Did you get the dinger?" Shelby asked, eyes wide.

"Oh, yeah," I said. "And we almost got caught so we had to hide out and sneak around until two o'clock."

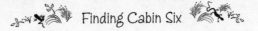

"Youch," Hayley said. "You must be really tired."

A thought dawned on me.

Johan's doing Survivor Day *this morning to get back at the dinger thieves.*

In less than five minutes, everyone was dressed, buffs in place, and ready to go. All except for Madison, who was still a lump in that purple paradise in her top bunk.

"Madison!" I shook the lump. "We gotta go! It's Survivor Day!"

Madison stirred, turned, and peeped out of her blankets, waving her white fleece blanket.

"I surrender."

I shook her some more. "NO! Don't you see? Johan's doing this on purpose to flush us out! We can't let him win!" I checked my watch. "Notice how he *didn't* ring the bell? That's because he couldn't without a dinger."

Madison popped her head out a little more, wiped her eyes with her hands, and smiled.

"Breakfast is in FIVE MINUTES! AND IT WILL BEHOOVE YOU TO EAT A LOT OF PANCAKES. You're gonna need the strength! HAHAHAHAHAHA!"

"He sounds hostile," Kayla said. "I'm scared."

"No need to be," I pulled the girls into a huddle. "We've got each other. And no matter what happens we have to promise not to give up any information about what happened to the dinger. Got it?"

Julia put her thumb and index finger together and pulled them across her lips like she was closing a zipper.

"They're not getting anything outta me."

The rest of the girls did the same.

"Great," I said. "Let's go eat and then win this Survivor Day."

The girls let out a yell and charged out the door toward the box. All except Madison.

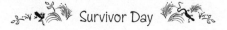

"C'mon, girl! I'm not leaving any friends behind."

Madison crawled out of her bed. She was still dressed in her clothes from last night, and her hair was frizzy and sticking up all over. I grabbed a hair tie off my shelf and helped her gather it in a high ponytail. Then I took her buff and pulled it over her head, using it as a wide headband. I stuffed her ponytail inside it.

"There. That'll keep the mud out of your hair."

Madison grinned. "Thanks."

I handed her another pair of my socks. "Here. There are a million more where those came from."

Madison sat down on my bed to slip the socks on. "My shoes are outside by the steps."

I grimaced. "Check 'em for crawly things before you put them on."

"Okay. Allie, do you really consider me a friend?"

Lord, help me answer this well.

I smiled. "Of course. You tend to bond with a person when you're shoved under a building with them for half a night."

It was a muddy Survivor morning. With tons of pancakes lodged like bricks in our guts, our teams competed in mud tug-o-wars, mud relays, mud runs, and mud fights. Lucky for us this was the day when the boys from Cabin Six were part of our team. By lunch time, we were ahead of the next best team by twenty-million points.

A water truck came along to spay us all down. The cool water felt great as the humid Louisiana day heated up.

Chef Gumbo and his staff had prepared a hot dog barbeque for us out on recreation field one. No way were they letting us inside with how messy we all were.

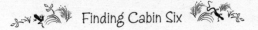

The great thing about picnics at Camp 99 Pines is you get to sit with whoever you want. And after we all went through the food line, the "Operation Dinger" team ended up sitting together in a circle in the shade on the sidelines of the field.

"Johan's looking over at us," Hunter said. "Do you think he suspects?"

"Keep your eyes in the circle, Hunter." Kendall pushed her brother's cheek to turn his head in a different direction. "Y'all were in your cabins when they blew Taps, and if he asks, you left your cabin to go to the bathroom 'cause that's what y'all did, right?"

"I'm a terrible liar," Ruby said.

"Ruby, this is a *camp* game. We call it *bluffin'.*"

"Then I'm a terrible bluffer."

"Then evade all questioning," Madison said. "Feign home-sickness or start scratching your bug bites. Anything to throw him off."

"He's comin' over here!" Kendall took a hot dog off her plate and shoved it in Ruby's mouth. "There. Now just keep chewin'."

"Well, hello, campers." Johan walked around our circle, his hands clasped behind his back. "This is rather odd. We've got members of . . . let's see . . . (he started flicking our buffs) Team Pinkeye, Lightning Rods, and Scarlet Fever—all havin' lunch *together*? That's not somethin' that normally happens on Survivor Day."

I swallowed a bite of potato chip and decided to call his bluff.

"Hey, I miss my cousins. We all got assigned to different cabins this year but we're trying to be good sports about it."

All true.

"And I actually *do* miss my twin brother sometimes." Madison grinned and punched Parker in the shoulder.

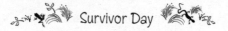

"Aww, Madi. You're the best." Parker reached over and pinched her cheek.

Johan walked around again, giving us all a raised eyebrow. He stopped at Nathan.

"You don't seem like you're from around here. What's your name?"

Nathan grinned and took a sip of his lemonade. "I'm from California." Then he stood and reached out a hand to shake Johan's. "My name's Nathan Fremont. Allie's brother Ryan is my science teacher and he invited me to come check out the camp. It's been great so far."

Man, that dude is charming!

And it seemed to work. Johan backed down.

"Well, I'm glad you're all having a nice lunch. What a strong, cohesive group you all seem to be!" Johan nodded his head and looked us over. "Well, that's gonna be important, ya know, 'cause this afternoon? It's gonna be tough . . ."

And then he turned and jogged away.

Kendall exhaled loudly.

"Whoa! That was stressful. He's got us figured out, I just know it."

Parker smiled and patted Kendall on the shoulder. "He's just bluffing, Kendall. Everything is going to be fine."

Kendall's face turned about the reddest I've ever seen it. Then she got up and started walking away.

"Gotta go scratch my bug bites."

I tried not to laugh. This had been such a crazy week. And it was only Tuesday.

It turned out to be the most strenuous Survivor Day afternoon

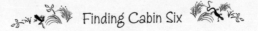

I had ever experienced. Each team was given a list of items located all over the camp that we had to find in two hours—like a scavenger hunt. The materials we were given to help complete the task consisted of a couple shovels, three potato sacks, two buckets, and a water bottle for each person.

"There are no rules except to stay off the west side of the property." Hawk was the one giving out the rules this time. "And stay away from snakes. DO NOT try to kill them. Unless you're a counselor."

We only had five minutes to formulate a strategy. The list of items to retrieve included heavy things, like heart and mushroom-shaped rocks, old anchors, and pieces of bench from the scrap pile that had specific words engraved on them. We also had to collect exactly five pounds of sand from the volleyball court, weighing it at a scale located on the porch of the nurse's hut. Then we needed to decipher clues to uncover five buried letters, bring all the items to the pool house, unscramble the letters to make a word, and carry our entire team and the items across the pool on a humongous pool float.

Oh, no! The pool?

"Okay, teams . . . time's up! On your mark, get set . . . go!"

Our strategy was to send Boys' Six and Four off to get the heavy stuff, and we girls took the shovels and clues to find the letters.

"Let's win this thing!" Blaze shouted, and the boys followed him, yelling a war cry.

"I'm glad we have Boys' Six with us today," Bliss said. "But it's gonna take us longer to get everyone across the pool."

"And we need to get there first so we can hide the dinger again," I said.

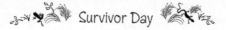

"I can't dig anymore!" Madison wiped her forehead with the back of her hand, smearing dirty grit across her freckles. Then she threw the shovel down.

"Ugh! I hate dirt!" She crumpled to the ground. "I'll never get it all off!"

Shelby grabbed the shovel, gave it a couple of tough pushes into the ground, and then we heard a click.

"Got the next letter!" Shelby grinned and Ruby, Hayley, and Julia reached into the hole to start digging the letter M out of the ground.

We laid it out next to the other four letters we had dug up: R, Y, E, C.

"Creamy?" Julia said.

"Not without an A." I scratched my head. "But I would sure love to eat something creamy right now."

"Ice cream." Madison still sat in a heap on the ground and whined, "Please find me some."

I reached out to grab her hand and lift her up. "Not yet, sister. First, we have to deliver these letters to the pool house and hope the Lightning Bolts and our Pinkeye brothers did what they were supposed to do." I checked my watch. "We've only got thirty minutes left."

We ran, slow and tired, but made it to the pool house in five minutes. Surprisingly, we were the first group to arrive.

Johan met us at the gate. He was holding up a round metal thing.

"You ladies know anything about this?"

I squinted and stepped a little closer to inspect the dinger. It had something scratched in it that I hadn't seen the night before.

Scratched into the center of the dinger was a familiar phrase—G6! *Note to self: Ask Mamaw if she ever stole the dinger out of the bell!*

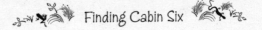

Seconds later, a huge group of dirty campers came running down the path toward the gate—some lugging sand-filled buckets and others with potato sacks weighed down with rocks, slung over their shoulders.

The Lightning Bolts from boys' Cabin Six led the pack.

But the Pinkeye boys weren't anywhere in sight.

And we needed our whole team to be there to get on the raft.

"Can I help with those?" Nathan took the letters from me and sorted them out on the pool deck.

Y—C—M—R—E.

Julia rearranged the letters.

C—R—E—M—Y

"See, I told you it wasn't Creamy."

Madison took a turn.

R—E—C—M—Y

"Wreck Me. That's it! That's what this camp is trying to do to me!"

"Check this out." Parker grabbed the M with his dirty hands, moved it to the front, and then adjusted some of the other letters.

M—E—R—C—Y.

Mercy. *That* was it.

"Yes! Maybe they'll finally show us mercy and let us quit this terrible game." Poor Madison. I'd never seen her so tired and frazzled.

Teams began shouting out their words. "Grace!" "Power!" "Risen!" "Alive!"

All great words. Ones I'm sure would be mentioned at tonight's campfire talk.

But first we had to get our raft across the pool.

Finally, the Pinkeye boys arrived. One boy had to drag his potato sack the whole way. He had found what had to be the biggest heart-shaped rock on the planet.

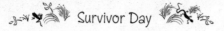

"Hey, it counts, right?"

"You bet," Johan said. "But unfortunately, your team will be the last to cross the pool."

Our only hope for points was if some of the other teams tipped over. And that hope was dashed in a matter of ten minutes, as Scarlet Fever, Hurricane 99, the Swamp Rats, and the Solar Flares all made it across—without anyone even getting so much as a foot in the water.

And then to add insult to injury, right as our team was almost settled and ready to float across the pool for last place, Dylan Sharpie—the biggest boy on Team Pinkeye—decided to do a cannonball onto the middle of the raft, sending all of us and most of the stuff splashing into the pool.

"We were losing anyway," was his reasoning.

It was a moment that would certainly be included in the end of the week video. But it was also a moment that could send Madison Doonsberry running to the camp office to call her dad to take her home.

I searched for her amid the splishing and splashing mayhem in the pool. I dove under the raft to make sure she wasn't drowning. I checked on all four sides—no Madison. And then I thought of something and checked the top.

There she was, holding on for dear life, hugging on to that huge heart rock that was anchoring everything down in the middle.

I pulled myself up, and climbed over to where she was, smiling, but with wet drippy hair poking out of her buff and hanging in her face.

"Did I survive Survivor Day?" she asked.

I laughed. "The competition part? Yes. But the 'day' isn't over."

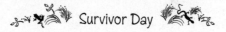

"Mercy, Grace, Power, Risen, Alive . . ."

Pastor Bo said the words slowly, carefully. "We don't want you to *ever* forget these words. That's why we had you dig them up and carry them around! We're going to talk about each of these words over the next few nights. But right now, let's focus on the first one—mercy. Anyone know what it means?"

"Mercy is when you choose to forgive and not punish someone—even when they deserve it." Great answer from Phoenix Ryan. He's a pastor's kid from my town. I think his dad pays him to know stuff like that.

"Like Dylan *deserved* a million noogies for sinking our raft?" Another boy—Max from Team Pinkeye—grabbed Dylan by the head and a few of his teammates started working him over with their knuckles.

Bo laughed. "Exactly right. Dylan deserves noogies! But you're not exactly extending mercy right now, are you?"

"Oh." Max let Dylan go. "I guess not. But . . ."

"But, what? He did a dumb thing? He lost points for the team? He got everyone wet? He dumped a bucket of sand in the pool and Ducky had to clean it all out?"

Dylan hung his head. "Oh, man, I'm sorry. I couldn't help myself. I guess I didn't think . . ."

Bo waved the comment off. "No big deal, Dylan. You're giving me a great illustration here."

Dylan straightened back up and grinned.

Bo continued. "Remember how we talked about sin last night and how it separates us from God? Well, here's what I want you to consider tonight. The apostle Paul—that same follower of Jesus we mentioned the other night, wrote this in a letter to his friend, Titus:

'When God our Savior revealed his kindness and

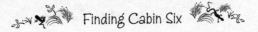

love, he saved us, not because of the righteous things we had done, but because of his mercy. He washed away our sins, giving us a new birth and a new life through the Holy Spirit.'"

Maestro got up and began strumming softly.

"Boys and girls, God wants to forgive your sins. He wants to bless you with his mercy. And you can ask for that right now and have a new life in Jesus Christ."

I watched Madison lean over to ask Bliss something. I was so excited for her. This would be her moment—I knew it. Today was the day she would become God's forgiven child. Finally.

Bliss nodded her head and Madison got up and walked away from the amphitheater.

What?

I scribbled a note and had Ruby pass it over to Bliss. Bliss scribbled a note and passed it back:

Where's Madison going?

To the bathroom.

No, she wasn't! Madison hates the bathhouse. She'd rather have her bladder explode than visit that place more than a couple times a day.

She didn't go to the bathroom.

She just escaped from God's invitation—that's what she did.

But why? Why would anyone run away from you, God?

I looked up at the sky and prayed for understanding, and right at that moment I saw a shooting star.

Don't worry, Allie. I'm going after her.

When we got back to the cabin later that night, there was a note attached to the ladder leading up to Madison's bunk.

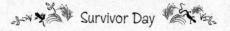

Sorry I left the talk. Exhausted. See you
all in the morning.

Hmmm. Yeah. I guess today had been a tiring day, especially after getting so little sleep the night before. Yes, that's what happened. She just needed her rest. The poor girl was spent.

"Good night, survivor," I said to the lavender lump on the top of the bed.

Then, a little later, after we had all brushed our teeth and Bliss turned out the last light, I heard, "Good night, friend."

CHAPTER 20

Water Day

"Water Day could quite possibly turn out to be my favorite day at camp," Madison said as she pulled her purple beach towel and purple-and-pink one-piece swimsuit out of her third suitcase. "No dirt, right? I can handle that." She stretched and yawned. "And I sure got a good night's sleep."

Tired girls slid off their bunks, not quite ready to start the day. I startled when I heard a familiar sound at 7:45—the bell!

"The dinger has been recovered!" Bliss laughed. "Imagine that! I wonder who took it."

Selective amnesia. That would be the key to surviving the rest of the week without giving away our secret.

Dinger? What dinger?

"Bathe in sunscreen today, girls. And put your swimsuit on now, with clothes over it for breakfast time since you may not have time to come back and change. See ya'll in the serving line!" Bliss bolted out of the cabin.

"Don't make eye contact with Johan at the box," I said. "We know nothing and we did nothing. Got it?"

I looked around at my Operation Dinger comrades. They nodded, pretended to zip their lips, and we headed off to the morning gathering.

"Good morning, campers!" Johan searched the crowd with a crazed glare. "And aren't you glad you weren't awakened by an airhorn this morning? Yes, our bell is back in action, and I need *your* help. It seems that a cabin—or several cabins—outsmarted

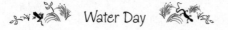

me, and I'm not a fan of LOSING. So, here's a deal for all of you: anyone who comes to me with solid evidence that proves who the dinger stealers are, will earn fifty-million points for their cabin. That's substantial, boys and girls."

Ugh. Remember you have amnesia, people.

"And even if it was *your* cabin, I'll still award you the points. Being cabin champs is that important. You'll get your names engraved on the Camp 99 Pines champ wall, you'll be able to sleep in the tree house the last night of camp, and all the staff will be making you the best last night feast you can imagine." He looked around the crowd again. "Any immediate takers?"

Everyone stayed quiet. I didn't even dare look at Girls' Five or Boys' Six. Even if I did want to wave at Nathan.

"Okay, then—my offer is good today *and* tomorrow. You can even write down your evidence and submit it anonymously. Just remember to write what cabin you're in."

He's raising the stakes. Not fair, Johan!

Even if we ratted ourselves out to get the points, it wouldn't keep Bliss and Blaze from being thrown in the swamp.

Everybody, just stay cool.

"Okay," Johan changed his countenance back to silly morning goofball. "Someone come up here and say a prayer for the day and for the food."

Ruby jumped up on the box. "Thank you, Lord, for keeping us all safe yesterday at Survivor Day and especially be with those who are still considering whether they should ask you into their lives. Thank you for our food, for Camp 99 Pines, and for an opportunity to be your servants today. In Jesus' name, amen."

We sang the Doxology, and this time Madison even belted out a few words. I wondered if she knew what "ye heavenly hosts" meant. Funny, I never realized how confusing things

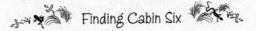

could be at a Christian camp until I started looking at them from Madison's point of view.

As we were being dismissed by cabin to go get breakfast, I spotted those three grownups again with my peripheral vision. Ellen, the realtor, Mr. Possible Camp Buyer Guy, and Patterson Gables.

It was already Wednesday. No more time to goof around.

I took a deep breath and ran over toward the trio.

"Good morning, Miss Ellen," I said, as I bounced over their way. "How are things going today?" I smiled and held my hand out to Mr. Gables. "Hello, Mr. Gables. How is your day shaping up?"

Patterson Gables stroked his mustache and scrunched his thick eyebrows together. "Little girl, why are you not with the other campers?"

"Oh, I'm sorry, it's just that I heard the camp was up for sale and . . ."

He didn't let me finish. "What is your name, young lady?"

"My name is Allie Carroway, sir."

He looked toward the sky, and did a little head roll. Then he grabbed the back of his neck and rubbed.

"You're not related to Katherine Carroway, are you?"

I nodded. "Katherine Carroway's my mamaw, although people just call her Kat."

Patterson groaned. "Oh, I'm sorry to hear that. Katherine Carroway is quite possibly the most dreadful person I've ever met."

"Patterson!" Mr. Buyer Guy piped up. Then he turned to me. "You'll have to excuse my friend. He's always grumpy in the morning. And I'm sure your mamaw's a delight."

"She is." Then I continued, barely taking a breath. "So, Mr. Gables, about the sale . . . don't you think it would be sad if

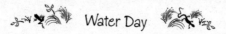

Camp 99 Pines didn't exist anymore? Would you consider selling it to someone else who would keep it a camp, if they could match your current offer?"

Patterson grimaced. "How *old* are you?"

"I'm thirteen, sir."

"Then I suggest you go back with the other thirteen-year-olds and let us adults take care of business. And for your information, so you don't have to wonder, I've accepted an offer from my friend Stan here and we plan to sign the final papers on Saturday afternoon. So, off you go! Eat some French toast and play your childish games."

Patterson turned and walked away and Ellen and Stan followed. Ellen gave me a sad face as she left, and Stan turned back to look at me and raised his palms in the air as if to say he couldn't do a thing to change the situation.

"Allie, are you okay??" Lola ran over to where I was standing alone, processing my frustration. "Were you just talking to those people?"

"Yep. Patterson Gables—the guy who's selling the camp. Ellen the realtor, and . . . Stan."

"Stan?"

"Yeah. And I think he might be the guy to help us."

French toast and bacon morning is my favorite. I ate three helpings. Water Day has a way of making you hungry fast so I prepared in advance.

After breakfast we hit the pool for raft relays, a water volleyball tournament, belly flop competition (which Hunter won!), and yes—the famous whirlpool. Every single camper is required to get in the pool for this. We all walk in the same

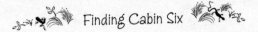

direction, until one of the lifeguards tells us to change direction. That's where the difficulty comes in. Water is powerful, and for a moment or two you just *can't* change direction. It's kind of like being in a water tornado with a hundred kids—and like a real tornado, things really get out of hand. And you can get hit with a hand. My cousins and I always link arms so at least we stay together and hopefully not run into creepy boys.

"Owww! I stubbed my toe on your knee!" Kendall reached down to rub her toe, and she disappeared under the water.

"Some people in this pool need to be introduced to the concept of a pedicure," Madison wailed after someone's toenails scraped her in the fray.

Lola and Ruby were laughing with their mouths open so soon they were choking out water.

"Change direction!" Ducky yelled.

So we tried and failed again. Some big kid actually floated over me—I don't even know how that happened. Kendall grabbed my swimsuit strap and accidentally pulled it off my shoulder.

"Kendall—don't expose me to the masses. I'd rather drown!"

Like I said, the whirlpool is scary.

The whirlpool also has a purpose. The counselors have never said this to us but I've figured it out. The whirlpool is just a big bath for kids who don't plan to shower all week. They always close the pool after the whirlpool. I think it's because they bring in boatloads of chlorine and a team of bacteria specialists to get the water clear again.

Yep. Scary.

At lunch, we gathered out on the lawn next to the pool house for another barbecue. This time it was burgers, and our "dinger group" spread out beach towels in a circle and rested in the shade.

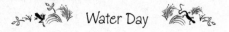

"I kicked a kid in the pool and chipped my toenail polish but besides that, this has been my favorite day of camp. Look, no dirt!" Madison sat with her legs stretched out in front of her, leaning back on her hands and staring up at the pine trees.

"It really is a shame they're selling this place." She turned to Parker. "Do you think Daddy has enough money to buy the camp?"

"I doubt it, Madison. Plus, he wouldn't know anything about running a camp—well, except for maybe the legal part."

Madison stared up at the sky some more. "Well, it's a shame it's going to go away. The place is growing on me a little."

Parker stood up and gathered some of our dirty paper plates and napkins to take to the garbage.

"Anyone want another Coke while I'm up?"

"Yeah, I'll take one," Hunter said. "That whirlpool made me thirsty!"

Parker smiled. "Be right back."

Parker balanced the trash in his arms and walked over to the bin near the edge of the lawn. Then he jogged over to the huge ice chest that was sitting by itself under a shade tree near the pool house gate. I watched him lift the lid, reach in, and then . . . he dropped to the grass and grabbed his right foot.

"Did Parker step on something?" I asked Kendall, since I knew *she* had been watching him.

Kendall jumped to her feet and shaded her eyes with her hand. "Somethin's wrong."

I jumped up too, and soon we heard Parker yell. "Blaze! Hawk! Help!" Then he slumped down on his side and began writhing around in the grass.

Blaze, Hawk, and Ducky beat us to Parker. Ducky held us away when we tried to crowd in.

"Radio Nurse Tammi," Blaze said to Ducky, "and have her call 9–1–1." Ducky sprinted to the pool house.

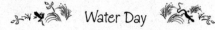

Hawk took out his machete that was attached to his belt and drove the blade into the ground a few feet away from us. Then he lifted two pieces of snake. "It's a copperhead. We gotta get this boy some help, fast."

And that's when Madison lost it.

"NO! Not my brother! Help him! Please, help him!" She began sobbing and screaming. "Help! Help!"

Parker reached up a hand. "Madi—you need to calm down, okay? That will help me a lot here."

"Does it hurt, Parker?" Madison changed from shouting to quiet crying.

"Yes, it hurts a lot." Then he groaned and lay back on the ground. Tears streamed down his face. He breathed heavily and began twisting and turning, like he was trying to get out of his skin. Sweat formed on his forehead and upper lip.

"Kids, please move away so he can have some air." Hawk threw the dead snake pieces down on the ground and kneeled, putting his face close to Parker's. "Parker, I need you to be as still as possible. That's going to slow down the spread of the venom. People get bit by copperheads all the time and survive. You're going to be okay."

At the sound of the word "venom," I got a little light-headed. Venom to me means poison, and poison is not a good thing to go into a person's body.

"Lord, help Parker. Please keep that venom from spreadin'."

Kendall had her eyes closed, but was praying out loud. She was also holding on tight to Madison, who had her hand over her mouth trying to muffle the noise from her sobs.

Blaze got up from where he was tending to Parker and used his arms to move people to each side to form a path.

"Here comes the medical team."

Two guys carrying a basket stretcher and a big medical pack ran up next to Parker.

"How are you doing, son?" the first guy said.

Parker could barely form words through his heavy breathing. "Not . . . so . . . good." He was shaking now, and his face was growing paler by the second.

The medical guys lifted Parker into the basket, placed a blanket on top of him, and ran out of there with him.

Ducky appeared out of the pool house with a walkie-talkie.

"They have an ambulance waiting down by the bell. They're calling his parents and will meet them at the hospital."

Madison ran forward. "Can I go? I'm his sister."

"Yes, you can."

Right about the time she said that, Bliss pulled up in a golf cart.

"Madison, Allie, get in. I'll drive you down there."

I don't know why she told me to get in, but I did what I was told. Madison and I hopped into the second seat and when we did Madison grabbed onto me.

And she didn't let go—all the way to the hospital.

Fighting for Life

It's because I'm a terrible person. That's why this is happening." Madison sat next to me in the emergency room, talking nonsense.

"What? You're not a terrible person. And this is happening because a copperhead slithered its way onto our field. It's Louisiana. Jesus Swamp Camp. You said it yourself on the first day."

"And if I had been a better daughter, my parents wouldn't be divorced, and my dad wouldn't have moved us to the swamp. And we wouldn't be at camp and Parker wouldn't have gotten bit. See, it all points back to me." Madison's cries had calmed, but her voice kept catching. "Parker's gonna die because of me."

Mamaw had been at Camp 99 Pines meeting with Miss Lindsey when Parker got bitten. She drove us to the hospital and now reached over and hugged Madison, rocking her back and forth.

"Sweet baby, none of what you just said is true. Jesus loves you, and he loves that twin brother of yours too. He's got his arms around him right now. You'll see, he's gonna be alright."

Madison closed her eyes, and tears flowed. A hospital attendant came over and brought a big, fluffy blanket to wrap around us since we were still wearing our swimsuits.

A few minutes later, Andrew Doonsberry—Parker and Madison's dad—came jetting through the door and approached the window.

"I'm Parker Doonsberry's father."

Immediately there was a buzz, and the doors to the ER popped open. Mr. Doonsberry disappeared.

Madison sniffed. "He didn't even see me."

"I'll go tell him you're here." Mamaw went to talk to the woman at the window, who buzzed her in too.

"Allie," Madison looked at me, big fat tears streaming down her cheeks, "my mom's in Paris. I'm all alone . . ."

"No, you're not. I'm here."

And Jesus is too. If you would only let him into your life.

I felt so sorry for Madison. Without faith in God, she was empty. Alone. Scared, with nothing to hang onto. She had no hope.

A couple of hours later, after Parker was stabilized and put in a regular hospital room, Madison, Mamaw, and I finally were able to get into the third-floor visitor's lobby. Mr. Doonsberry came out to comfort Madison and tell us that while Parker was very sick, he was going to survive. They just needed to monitor him closely overnight.

And Bliss had arrived with some clothes for Madison and me to change into.

"We gathered all the kids in the camp to pray for your brother, Madison." She handed us some jeans, T-shirts, and clean socks and shoes. "Everyone sends their love."

Madison grinned for the first time in many hours. "Thanks, Bliss. I'm so glad you were my counselor."

"I told you—I've been prayin' for you girls for *three* years! And I'm *still* your counselor. You'll be back at camp tomorrow. God's not through with you yet, girl!"

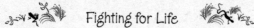

Madison shook her head. "Oh, no. I'm not going back until I'm sure Parker's okay. I haven't even seen him yet."

"He's gettin' there, darlin'," Mamaw said. "Right now he needs some rest, a little medicine, and a lotta prayer. Your daddy said you could come spend the night at my house with Allie, since her parents are out of town tonight. We'll check on your brother in the mornin' and if all is well, I can drive you and Allie back to camp. How does that sound?"

Madison nodded. "I'd like that."

Mamaw smiled. "I'll make you some good old comfort food too. Now, for heaven's sake, you two go put some clothes on!"

CHAPTER 22

Prayer Barn

It was seven o'clock by the time we arrived at Mamaw and Papaw's house, and we were starving. Thankfully, Mamaw always has food prepared, so she heated up some chicken and dumplings and mac & cheese, and set us up at the kitchen counter to eat.

"You girls will feel much better after you get that in your system." Mamaw sliced some cinnamon-streusel cake for dessert. We gobbled it all down in minutes.

Then Mamaw braided Madison's and my hair—*after* she brushed all the tangles out. We hadn't had time to even think about our hair, and it was still in a post whirlpool mess.

While she was braiding, I decided to ask her a question.

"Mamaw, when you were a camper at 99 Pines, did you ever take the dinger out of the bell?"

Mamaw froze and looked at me with a straight face.

"Allie-girl, have *you* ever taken the dinger out of the bell?"

I tried another one.

"Do you know what happened to girls' Cabin Six?"

Mamaw kept her straight face. "Do *you* know what happened to girls' Cabin Six?"

I was going to just keep asking questions, but then Madison piped up.

"Mamaw Kat, we found the original foundation of girls' Cabin Six! It was under the girls' visitor lodge. It has a big circle with G6 carved in the concrete."

Mamaw resumed braiding. "Are you sure it said G6? And what were y'all doin' under the girls' lodge?"

Uh-oh. Better ask another question.

"Mamaw, have *you* ever been under the girls' lodge?"

Mamaw chuckled. "Seems we all have information that we're not willin' to give up just yet."

"Camp secrets are sacred," I said. "We have people to protect from the Allibeaver."

"So do I," Mamaw said. "But it's all in fun, right?"

"Well," Madison frowned. "I was starting to think so, until my brother got bit by a copperhead."

Mamaw finished up Madison's braids, and it made her look a little like my cousin Ruby. Sweeter, calmer, and a whole lot less dramatic.

"Speakin' of Parker," Mamaw said, "let's go pray for him right now."

Mamaw disappeared into the hallway and brought back two of her most cozy fleece blankets. Then she poured some hot cocoa in mugs, put them on a tray, and handed it to me.

"I think the Prayer Barn would be a nice place to go. It's gonna be dark soon. You'll be able to see some stars through the top windows."

We walked out the front door, down the steps from the porch, and then hiked a few more steps to the Prayer Barn on the side of the house.

"This place *is* nice," Madison said as she entered the Prayer Barn, and she plopped down on one of the comfy brown sofas. She looked around at the many shelves. "You have a lot of books."

"Mamaw has *lots* of rooms filled with books. This is just one of them. The Bible I gave you came from in here," I said. "When I was younger, I used to spend hours in this place, reading, and

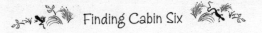

looking out at the river through that window." I pointed to the lower, rectangular window. "And then at night, I would look out at the stars through that window."

"What a unique window design," Madison said, and then she craned her neck to look around. "And it's the same on these other two walls too? Interesting."

"Girls, it's been a long day, and I'm gettin' tired. Let's pray for Parker, and then you can stay out here for as long as you want."

Mamaw grabbed my hand and brought me over to the sofa where Madison was sitting. She sat in the middle of us, put her arms around our shoulders, and began to pray.

"Dear Father in Heaven, we bring dear, sweet Parker to you right now. Lord, he needs your strength, comfort, and healing. Please help the doctors know what to do and give him a good, restful night's sleep. Put your angels around him to protect him. We trust you, Lord. And please, help Madison know just how much you love her and how you care about everything she is going through. In Jesus' name, amen."

Mamaw reached over and gave both of us a big hug. "Okay, Papaw and I will be in the house if you need anything." She kissed us both on the forehead. "You are loved," she said, and then she walked out the door.

I jumped back over to the other sofa, put my blanket over me, and sipped my hot cocoa.

"You're very lucky," Madison said, "to have a Mamaw like that."

"Yeah, she's pretty special."

"And to think she fills up rooms and rooms of books for all the grandkids? You'll probably never have time to read everything."

I chuckled. "Yeah, we've tried. But you're right, it's a never-ending supply of blessings. She likes to share."

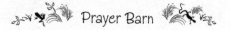

Madison lowered her mug to her lap and tipped her head back on the cushy arm of the sofa to look out the top window. "Stars are coming out."

I smiled. "They're gonna get real bright soon."

"Can we sleep out here tonight? It kinda reminds me of Cabin Four in here and I know this sounds ridiculous, but I miss it, just a little."

I laughed. "Sure, I don't think Mamaw would mind."

And then I heard that little God-voice, nudging me to do something uncomfortable—again.

Talk to her about me.

I took a deep breath.

"Madison, why did you leave the campfire the other night? Were you really tired or were you running away because Bo was talking about Jesus?"

Madison didn't move from her position. She kept staring out the window.

"I was running away."

I sat up. "Really? Why?"

"Oh, come on, Allie. You should be able to figure it out. I'm a terrible person. I've done too many bad things. I figured that God could never forgive *me*, and that made me sad. I had to get out of there before I lost it."

Now Madison was sitting up. She drained the last of her cocoa and set the mug on the end table.

"Madison, God forgives *everyone* who asks."

"Yeah, but what if I don't *want* him to forgive me? I feel like I deserve to be punished."

"For what? What could be so bad?"

Madison huffed and puffed a couple of times. "I hurt *you*, Allie. Don't you remember? 'Frenelope'?"

Of course, I remembered. Frenelope was an anonymous

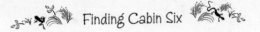

girl who stole my cousin Lola's phone at Madison's birthday party. She downloaded a video of me doing a skit for my family that made fun of Miss Lewis—a teacher no one liked at school. She posted it on social media, and the video went viral. It almost got me removed as Student Project Manager of the year-end fundraiser and carnival at school.

"I'm Frenelope," Madison admitted. Then she covered her face with both hands and rested her elbows on her lap.

That video going viral was one of the most humiliating moments of my life. How am I supposed to respond, Jesus?

Madison put her hand out.

"And that's *not* all. Remember when Mr. Felix didn't show up at the dog training event, and you called him, and he was in New Orleans and said that someone had called during the week to cancel?"

I was speechless. I knew what was coming.

"*That* was me too." Madison started crying again. "Allie, I'm *so* sorry."

So now I knew for sure what I had suspected all along. Madison Doonsberry had been trying to destroy my reputation and ruin the year-end school fundraising event.

But why?

It really doesn't matter now. Just love her.

I didn't say anything for a minute or two. I had to wait for my thoughts to catch up with my emotions, so that my emotions wouldn't cause my body to do something I would regret. Love her? Why? She had shown NO love for me.

But God showed his great love for us by sending Christ to die for us while we were still sinners. Romans 5:8

My Bible memory verses have a way of popping up when I least expect them. And I kind of wanted to ignore this one right now.

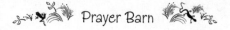

What she did to me was awful, God.

Madison jumped to her feet. "See! I told you! I don't deserve forgiveness from you *or* from God! That's why I ran away from the campfire!"

Madison threw her blanket on the sofa and wiped tears off her cheeks with the palms of her hands. Then she headed toward the door.

"Wait. Where are you going?"

She fumbled with the doorknob. "I don't know. Just leave me alone."

I grabbed her blanket off the sofa. "But you can't keep running away, Madison."

"Watch me." She finally pulled the wooden door open and began to push her way out the screen door.

I had to stop her. And all I could think of was to throw the blanket! It landed perfectly, like a net over her head, covering her body down to her knees.

"ALLIE!"

Madison thrashed around and I grabbed her and pulled her down and back, onto the floor of the Prayer Barn. She kicked and punched but the blanket absorbed all the blows.

"Let me GO!" she yelled, and we wrestled around for a few seconds. I had an advantage since my arms and legs were free and I managed to wrap her up tighter in the blanket and sit on top of her so she couldn't move.

"UGH!" Madison screamed. "LET ME GO!!!!"

"NO!" I yelled back. "I'm NOT going to let you go. Not till you let me tell you something."

She stopped struggling and was quiet for a second.

"O . . . kay. But can you at least uncover my head?" The muffled voice made me giggle to myself.

"Only if you promise to hear me out."

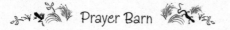

"I promise."

I stood up, and released Madison from the blanket. Her braids were no longer nice and neat. Hair was sticking out everywhere, standing on end because of the blanket static. I noticed that her bruise from the David and Goliath incident was turning a new and exciting shade of . . . avocado green.

Madison stared at me. "Okay, I'm listening."

I chuckled. "Come sit down, please."

Madison rolled her eyes and slinked to the sofa.

I sat down next to her.

"Madison, I forgive you for everything."

She shook her head. "No. You can't do that. I won't let you."

"Ha! You can't decide that." I pushed my thumb into my chest. "I get to decide that."

"Then I won't accept it."

"THERE!" I pointed at her. "That's your problem! You won't accept God's forgiveness either. You're such a stubborn . . ."

Madison looked at me with wide eyes, hands on her hips. "A stubborn what?"

"A . . . a . . . stubborn SHEEP!" I crossed my arms. "You're a stubborn sheep. Stop running away from love, Madison. God's not going to stop going after you. And neither am I. So just STOP."

And then something happened. I didn't hear anything or see anything. But I felt something. I think it was Madison's heart opening up.

Night had fully arrived so we sat in the dark, moon and starlight shining in from those upper windows. I kept my mouth shut, moved to the other sofa, and just prayed that this stubborn but loved, lost sheep would finally be returned to the fold so we could celebrate—like the guy in Jesus' parable.

Jesus, she needs you.

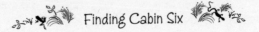

A few quiet minutes passed—Madison laying on her sofa and me sitting on mine. Then, she finally moved. She stood up, turned around, got on her knees, bowed her head, and clasped her hands.

Then she looked over at me. "I don't know what to say to him."

I smiled. "Tell him that. And then whatever comes to your heart."

She bowed her head again. "Dear God, I don't know what to say. I have a hard time believing that you love me. But I want to. Will you please forgive me . . . for everything? I want to be your child. I want to follow you. I want you to be my Savior. So, please, will you help me?"

She knelt there for a while and tears streamed down both our faces. Then she finally got up, lay down on the sofa, and pulled the blanket up to her chin.

I did the same on my side of the room.

"Allie . . ."

"Yeah."

"I think that prayer worked."

I smiled. "I know it did."

CHAPTER 23

Daytime Discovery

We slept for a long time. I know, because the sun was coming in the top windows when we finally woke up.

"Arrrgh. Blinded!" I covered my eyes with my forearms, and rolled over to face Madison. "Are you alive over there?"

Madison sat up and stretched. "Yeah. Barely. What time is it?"

I fumbled on the end table to find my sports watch. "Eleven o'clock!"

"What? Wow. I think this sofa is more comfortable than my bed!"

"It probably is. I come out here and sleep a lot."

Madison put her clasped hands behind her head and looked up at the ceiling and then all around at the walls of the Prayer Barn.

"I can't get over how they put those bookshelves in between each of the long windows. When did your grandparents build this place?"

"I don't know. It's been here as long as I have."

"Did it always have the shelves? Because it looks like this room was designed for a different purpose. I can't stop thinking about the unique window design."

"I guess I never thought about that. I just know that I like the windows a lot. They give me a nice view of the property and a lot of natural light for reading."

"Hmmm." Madison flipped the blanket off, got up, and

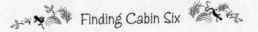

walked around. She ran her finger up and down book spines and along the window ledges. She checked out some of the dents in the wooden walls and jumped up and down a couple of times. Then she stood on tip-toes and raised her hand to touch the top windows. Then she walked over to the door and opened it.

"Hey—you're not going to try to escape again, are you?"

"Oh, no. I'm not interested in being beat down by a blanket again. It's just . . ."

Madison opened the screen door next but then closed it. She turned and looked back inside the cabin for a moment, and then . . . .

"ALLIE!"

Her squeal made me jump to my feet.

"What?"

"Look around this Prayer Barn . . . carefully! Do you feel like you've been in a similar place lately? Like during *this* week?"

"The only place I've been all week is camp. Oh, and the hospital."

"Yeah. I'm not talking about the hospital."

"Okay, then camp?"

"Yeah. Think about our LIVING QUARTERS."

I looked around. It was rustic, yet cozy. I walked over to where Madison stood by the door.

"I guess it seems a little bit like our cabins at Camp 99 Pines."

Madison raised her eyebrows. "A *little* bit?" Madison grabbed my cheeks and turned my head in different directions. "Look again." Then she moved toward a side wall. "Let me help you. Imagine that instead of a bookshelf, you have a bed here, right next to this window. Then imagine you're climbing a ladder to a top bunk—oh, look at that. It *also* has a window. And

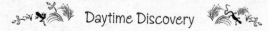

then imagine blinds on all these windows. And right here—" Madison jumped to the middle of the room and pointed to a place in the middle of the floor. "Right here, imagine a pink, fluffy rug that says, 'Welcome to the Palace'."

My heart started to pound and my head got a little light.

"What are you saying, Madison?"

Madison crossed her arms and stuck out her right hip. "I'm not going to say a thing until I go check something."

She ran for the door, but I got there first. I threw open the screen and we elbowed each other going down the stairs. Then we tore around to the back of the Prayer Barn, which happens to sit on blocks on top of a concrete foundation. We knelt next to the left back corner of the familiar wood building. I put my hand out to feel for a little carved circle.

Sure enough, there it was.

We both pulled our heads in close to look at the circle.

And yes, it had a G6 in the middle of it!

"Okay," Madison got a rascally grin on her face. "*Now* I'll say it. Allie Carroway, we have found girls' Cabin Six!"

CHAPTER 24

Fishin' For Answers

Our amazing discovery pumped enough adrenaline in our systems to give us energy to get dressed, do our hair, and get over to the main house to eat breakfast. Then we asked Mamaw to take us to the hospital to visit Parker and then back to camp.

"Well," Mamaw said from the driver's seat in her Jeep, "it was sure nice seeing Parker sittin' up and eatin' with some color back in his cheeks. I told you God was watchin' out for him."

Madison and I sat in the back seat, gesturing wildly to each other and even writing notes on some old church bulletins we found in the pockets on the backs of the seats.

Madison wrote and handed me a paper.

Are you gonna say anything?

I nodded and then said something.

"Mamaw, I just realized we're gonna be late for your alumi tour. I'm sorry."

Madison rolled her eyes at me, and scribbled.

That's NOT what I meant.

Mamaw looked back at me in the rear view.

"Allie-girl, I don't need a tour. I practically built the place."

"Did you help build the cabins?" Madison blurted out.

Mamaw laughed. "No. I didn't *actually* build anything, sweetheart. I just meant I was around when a lot of this camp was built up. Remember, I was here the first year it opened so I've seen a lot of changes."

"You were in high school that first year, right, Mamaw?"

"Yeah. Summer after tenth grade. And I met two *very* nice boys that year. Their names were Saul and Ray."

"Uncle Saul and Papaw Ray?"

"Yep. We had some fun competin' against each other for cabin champs that year. We beat them out by one-million points. And our cabin got to sleep in the tree house on the last night. I love how traditions pass on from generation to generation."

Madison glared at me and scribbled.

ASK HER!

I kept silent. But Madison didn't.

"Mamaw Kat, what cabin were you in that year?"

Mamaw flipped on her right turn signal.

"Oh, look, girls, here we are! Isn't it great to be back at Camp 99 Pines?" She pointed to a group of women near the nurse's hut. She moved her head closer to the windshield.

"Oh, my heavenly days, I know those old ladies!"

Mamaw screeched the tires and pulled into a parking place. "Come with me, girls, and I'll introduce you to some real characters!"

Madison and I piled out and had to jog to keep up with Mamaw. She had both her arms spread out to her sides as she ran toward the circle of ladies.

"Heeeeeeeey! Emma! Betsy!"

The group turned toward Mamaw. The one with the green glasses yelled, "Kat Clark? Is that you?"

Then the squealing and hugging began. A few other names like Pearl, Sandra, and Bonnie got thrown around. I couldn't tell which one was which.

Madison and I stood there just outside the squealing circle.

"Clark? Is that your Mamaw's maiden name?" Madison had to scoot back so she wouldn't get knocked over by the hugging ladies.

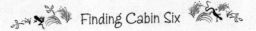

"Yeah. I have a hard time thinking that she wasn't always a Carroway."

Madison smiled. "She kept the same initials when she got married? KC, right? Very helpful when you own monogrammed items."

Figures Madison would think of that.

"Allie-girl and Madison, I want to introduce you to some of my best friends in the whole world." Mamaw beamed as she gestured to the sweet, older ladies who all seemed to have the same spunky grin as Mamaw.

"We were cabinmates the first year here at Camp 99 Pines. This is Patsy, Bonnie, Lily, Pearl, Rose, Sandra, Emma, and . . ."

"AUNT BETSY!" Bliss yelled that as she came flying over toward the nurse's hut. The lady who hadn't yet been introduced turned around and Bliss wrapped her up in a big hug.

"I'm guessing that's Betsy?" I said to Mamaw.

Betsy had to push Bliss off her so she wouldn't get strangled. Then, with a strong, but out-of-breath, voice, she introduced her great-niece.

"This is my lovely Elizabeth. She was named after me. Don't we look alike?"

Well, they didn't really look alike now, but I remembered that scrapbook picture, and they were identical when they were the same age.

"Elizabeth?" Madison grinned. "*That's* your real name?"

Bliss shrugged. "Yeah. But I'm Bliss at camp. Remember that, girls."

"Oh, that's such a wonderful camp name," Betsy said. "I would have picked that one for you! Elizabeth brings such joy and happiness wherever she goes." She pointed an index finger in the air. "But . . . she has a rascally side."

"Yeah, we know," Madison said.

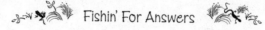

"She sounds a lot like our Goldie." The lady, who I think was named Pearl, went over and gave Bliss a hug. "It's so nice to meet you, finally."

"Goldie?" I looked at the circle of women. Their smiles faded a bit.

"Dear, sweet Goldie," Pearl said. "I miss her."

"Who's Goldie?" Madison asked, before I got a chance to stop her.

The lady with the denim jacket and cute red sneakers—Emma—spoke up. "Goldie was our counselor."

Emma then spied something behind us, and her dimmed smile turned to a scowl. "Don't look now, but here comes the scoundrel himself."

We all turned to see the now notorious threesome—Ellen, Stan, and Patterson Gables—approaching our circle.

"Well, hello, Patterson." Mamaw stepped into the middle of the circle, which had now become more like a horseshoe. "It's so good to see you."

Ellen and Stan took off toward the mess hall but Patterson came and stood right next to me.

"Katherine Carroway, to what do I owe this unfortunate meeting?"

Mamaw laughed. "Oh, Patterson. You have such a gift for sarcasm! Your sweet mother invited me to the 50th year anniversary gala. I'm here to celebrate all the amazing things God has done on this property. I'm sure you agree, don't you, that God is in charge and has plans for this place?"

The older women all stared him down.

Patterson's shifty eyes worked hard not to look at any of them.

He took his glasses off and rubbed his right eye. "Oh, yes, I agree. And it seems that God is closing the door on Camp

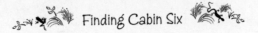

99 Pines. But, you know, I bet many Christian families will pay good money to build their dream houses here. Perhaps some of them will be our camp alumni. I can see it now. You can buy a house on the same block as some of your old cabinmates . . ." Patterson put his glasses back on and smirked.

"Patterson Gables! You used to be fun and adventurous. When did you become a stuffy old goat?"

Whoa, Aunt Betsy has a little bit of snark to her.

"Patterson," Mamaw interrupted. "I'd like you to meet my granddaughter, Allie, and her friend Madison."

Patterson raised one eyebrow. "Yes, I have met your grand-daughter. She's *just* like you, Katherine."

Mamaw smiled. "Yes, I know. And it thrills me to no end."

"And speaking of 'ends,' I'm afraid I must end this conversation. I have a meeting with my buyer. But, please know"—Patterson put his hand on his heart—"my heart is breaking to leave you, ladies."

"Oh, you'll see us again," Aunt Betsy said. "You can bet on that."

Patterson stuck his tongue out like he was gagging and strode away toward the mess hall.

"Well, Kat," Emma said, "I guess he's still mad at you for breaking up with him."

"But," Betsy added, "we can all tell that PG still hearts KC." Then she nudged Mamaw with her elbow.

The old ladies all giggled.

"Stop this nonsense." Mamaw laughed. "Stop it right now."

PG ♥ KC? *Like from the old bench that is now my bed*?

No way.

CHAPTER 25

S.O.S.

Mamaw and her cabinmates decided to take their own tour of the camp and I was pretty sure no staff person on the grounds would have the nerve to stop them. And since Madison and I found no one around to clue us in on the camp schedule for the afternoon, we had to make our way to the bulletin board near the box to find out where our people were.

Madison ran her finger down the list of weekly activities until she came to Thursday afternoon.

"Says here it's an all-camp David and Goliath—again. I used up all my deceit the other day, Allie. And my head finally isn't sore. Can we please find something else to do?"

Just then, a parade of kids from Team Pinkeye came walking in our direction.

"How's Parker?" Ruby asked. "I've been praying for him, non-stop."

"Thanks, Ruby," Madison said. "He's going to survive. But I'm sure he'll never go barefoot in the swampy grass ever again."

"Where are you all going?" I noticed that a couple of the boys carried buckets and some of the girls had plastic caddies filled with glass spray, sponges, and rolls of paper towels.

"Well," Hayley sighed. "Boys' Cabin Four received the PIG AWARD for the third day in a row!" She glared at the boys on our team.

The Pig Award is not a good thing. The Pig Award is given

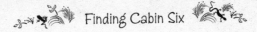

to the messiest cabin in camp. And you lose points for your team if you get it.

"And so," Julia continued, "Team Pinkeye has been assigned an S.O.S. for the afternoon so we can earn our points back."

"Does that mean we don't have to play David and Goliath?" Madison's eyes brightened.

"No, it means that we don't *get* to play David and Goliath," Dylan Sharpie said.

Madison put her hands on her hips. "Well, Mr. Cannonball, far be it for you to complain. If your cabin looks anything like what you did to the pool the other day . . ."

"Team Pinkeye! There you are!" Miss Lindsey came jogging over to our sorry looking little group. "I hear you have an S.O.S. I'm so happy to have some extra cleaning and setting up help today. We have a big event coming up tomorrow, you know."

The gala. I need to figure out how to get into that.

Miss Lindsey rubbed her hands together. "They're delivering all the tables and chairs out to recreation field two right now and they're dirty. So, I need you to go and clean them up."

I remembered what Miss Lindsey's letter had said about the gala.

Three hundred in attendance.

That's a lot of tables and chairs. It was going to be a long afternoon.

"Now, if y'all do a good job, you'll get your points back. Before that Pig Award, Team Pinkeye was in the lead, and girls' Cabin Four, you had the most points in the whole camp." Miss Lindsey smiled at Madison. "I hear your brother is recovering nicely. Hawk already has his snakeskin up on a plaque."

Madison hugged herself and shivered. "I never want to see that thing again."

Miss Lindsey hugged Madison. "I understand. That must

have been so scary for you. But I hope you've had a good week besides that."

Madison grinned and looked over at me. "It's been . . . uncomfortably amazing," she said.

For all of us.

"Okay, then, let's get out there and scrub!" Miss Lindsey led us out to recreation field two. Some men were working to put up a big white tent in the middle of the field so we had to stay close to the sides to wash down the rented white chairs and tables.

After about thirty minutes, Miss Lindsey pulled me and Madison aside.

"I have another job that will be perfect for both of you." Miss Lindsey winked. "How would you like to sort through and set up the silent auction items?"

That sounded much better than having prune fingers for the next two hours.

Miss Lindsey took us to the camp office where loads of interesting items had been piled up and down the hallways.

"I didn't know you were having a silent auction too." I picked up a small wooden sign that was a replica of the Camp 99 Pines sign that sits at the entrance.

Miss Lindsey lowered her voice. "Well, the camp board has not given up hope that Mr. Gables will change his mind and either keep the camp or sell it to us. We have *some* money, but we need more to be able to make a reasonable offer. Having an auction is our best shot at raising the rest of the funds. It worked fifty years ago, when the Gables' needed to raise insurance money to keep the camp open."

"How exactly does a silent auction work?" Madison asked.

Miss Lindsey went to her desk and picked up a stack of card stock. "Well, all the items and services donated will be

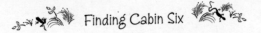

displayed on tables, and during the gala, people can make bids—the amount they would like to pay for the item—by writing the amounts and their names down on these forms. When the auction time is up, the name that has the largest bid next to it will be the person who 'wins' the item. They'll have to pay us before they take the item home, so tomorrow night—Lord willing—we may end up with enough money to buy the camp."

I reached down to pick up what looked like a picture frame with a gift certificate in it.

"One week at a beachside home in Maui? Someone donated this?"

Miss Lindsey nodded. "We have some very generous people who love Camp 99 Pines."

Madison got a huge smile on her face. "I could ask my daddy if he could donate some signed *Lunker Law* souvenirs."

"I might just let you use the phone for that," Miss Lindsey said.

"And I can call our wardrobe director and see if she can bring some of the camo gear I've worn on the show. I bet some people would buy it for their daughters or granddaughters."

"Everything helps, Allie. But don't forget to pray! We need that more than anything."

"Prayer is a pretty neat thing," Madison said.

For two hours, Madison and I wrapped auction items in cellophane, made fabric bows, filled in forms for each item, and grouped them in categories: gift cards, service certificates, trips, souvenirs, and an extra special category—Camp 99 Pines Memorabilia. That category had some cool stuff in it. Paintings on old bench wood, crosses that had been placed

around camp over the years, murals of each years' themes, and even old Camp 99 Pines T-shirts.

"I wish I could be at the gala and bid on some of these things." I pulled out the last of the tape from a roll. "Whoops! Need more supplies."

Madison and I took a break and went to the counselor's supply room to get more tape. And that's where we saw Parker's copperhead—well, the skin—proudly displayed with the rest of the "snakes" on the wall.

I walked up and ran my finger across the checkered skin. "God was really watching out for him," I said. Above the skin was a Scripture, written in permanent marker:

No, despite all these things, overwhelming victory is ours through Christ, who loved us.

Romans 8:37

"Check this out, Madison. Every snake has a Bible verse to go with it." I laughed. "Way to go, Hawk!"

Madison shook her head. "You Christians can be *so* weird sometimes."

"Hey, don't you mean *we* Christians?" I gestured between the two of us.

Madison got a funny look on her face. "Yes. I guess I do mean we."

On our way back with the new roll of tape we ran into Mamaw and her old cabin friends.

"Hi, girls! Do y'all need help with your S.O.S.? We heard about the Pig Award. Sorry about those stinky boys messin' things up."

"You can come and help us make some bows," I said. "Mine are all crooked, and Madison can't seem to choose any color except purple."

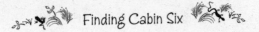

Madison reached over and pushed me off balance a little.

They followed us into Miss Lindsey's office, that was now overflowing with wrapped silent auction items.

Pearl gasped. "This brings back memories of the silent auction we had that first year."

Betsy put a hand to her chest. "I'm holdin' back tears right now."

"Do you suppose there's gonna be a 'silent' silent auction too?"

"Emma . . ." Mamaw put her index finger up to her lips.

"I'm sorry, Kat."

"Don't fret about it. Let's just get the rest of these items wrapped." Mamaw reached down and pulled some ribbon and scissors from a plastic bag on the floor. As she straightened up she caught me looking at her. I was giving her the Carroway "raised eyebrow," which means—*you're hiding something, and I'm gonna find out what it is.*

I already found Cabin Six.

And what's a 'silent' silent auction, Mamaw?

CHAPTER 26

Helping Hands

I couldn't wait until dinnertime. That was when I would see all my cousins—and I was busting at the seams with information about, well . . . everything.

"Madison, save me a seat next to you. I'll be there soon."

I darted back and forth between the girls' Cabin Five table and the boys' Cabin Six. I grabbed up Lola, Kendall, and Hunter. And—oh, yeah, I almost forgot—Ruby, from my cabin!

"Meet me at the box. I have information that could help us save the camp!"

"But, I'm hungry," Hunter said, as he looked down at his plate of fried chicken and tater tots.

"Stuff it in your pockets and bring it with you. This is important!"

In five minutes, we had all snuck out of the mess hall and were sitting cross-legged on top of the box. I showed them the "PG ♥ KC" rubbings I had made from my repaired bed wood, and I told them about the discovery of the girl's Cabin Six foundation. Then I told them how we found out that girls' Cabin Six was actually Mamaw's Prayer Barn.

Kendall gasped. "I knew somethin' was special about that place!"

I also filled them in on how there had been a silent auction the first year of Camp 99 Pines so they could raise insurance money to keep the camp running.

And I told them how Emma—Mamaw's former cabinmate

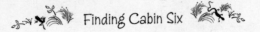

in Cabin Six—had accidentally mentioned a "silent" silent auction and how Mamaw had shushed her.

"Something went down at that auction. I don't know what but I think all the girls in Cabin Six were involved."

"Whoa. It's a full-on mystery," Hunter said as he popped a tater tot in his mouth.

"We've got to get ourselves into that gala tomorrow night," I said.

"But how?" Ruby asked. "We're just campers."

I covered my face with my hands and wracked my brain for ideas.

Lord, will it help for us to be there? If so, give me an idea.

I popped my head up.

"I've got it! I know how we can get to the gala!"

"I'm in, no matter what it is," Hunter said.

"Us too." Lola put her arms around both Kendall and Ruby.

"Okay, here's the plan. We'll just have to pray it works. Tomorrow morning three cabins have to tie for the Pig Award."

I filled Madison and our cabinmates in on the plan as we were getting ready to go to the campfire talk.

"You want us to *mess up* our princess cabin? I don't know if I'm physically able to do that." Madison looked like she was going to cry.

"Our only chance is to get an S.O.S. I know they're going to need help at the gala. We'll ask if we can pour water, serve, scrape plates in the kitchen—whatever."

"I think we should have the boys scrape plates," Madison said.

Kendall laughed. "I bet Hunter would be happy to take care of the leftovers."

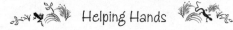
"Should we tell Bliss about all this?" Ruby asked. "I don't want her to be disappointed in us for messing up the cabin."

"Hmmm. Let me think about that. She knows about the missing cabin, *and* she's been hanging out with her Aunt Betsy all day. I bet she would like to be part of our little caper . . ."

"Alive. That's our word for tonight. If you asked Jesus into your heart this week, you are now spiritually alive."

I glanced over at Madison. She had Mamaw's Bible open to 2 Corinthians, watching Bo intently, and she had a peaceful grin on her face.

Thank you, God.

"Take a look at chapter five, verse 17. The apostle Paul wrote this: 'Anyone who belongs to Christ has become a new person. The old life is gone. A new life has begun.'"

Madison scribbled on her note pad, and though I couldn't see what she wrote, I'm sure it wasn't a note asking permission to leave this time.

Bo continued, "But I know you're probably thinking, 'Hey, Bo, I don't feel so new. In fact, I still have all the same problems I had before I accepted Christ. And those problems stink almost as much as boy's Cabin Four! What should I do about that?'"

Ha! Good one, Pastor Bo.

Maestro jumped up on the platform and began strumming his guitar. And our counselors all got up and grabbed big rolls of craft paper from the floor on the stage.

"Here's what we're going to do about those stinky problems—but only if you want to. We're going to spread these papers all around the amphitheater and give you some pens. Outline one of your hands. Then—only if you want to—write

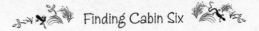

that problem down inside the hand. Then hand it to God. After a few minutes, you'll move to a different hand. Read what it says, put your hand on top of it, and pray for that person to *really* give it to God. He's the *only* one who knows exactly what to do."

The music played and the counselors spread the papers out. Kids got up, slowly. But eventually—one by one—they each found a pen and a spot. I chose a spot that wasn't near any of my friends or cousins—or that cute boy from California.

Just me and you, God. Thanks for this time. I love this camp.

I outlined my hand, and then while I talked some more with God I drew myself some fingernails. Colored them in. Then I drew knuckle wrinkles.

Now what?

I closed my eyes and prayed. Then I let the pen go. And this is what I wrote:

Help me love people like you love them.

And . . .

Please save Camp 99 Pines. I can't do it.

That's a hard thing for me to admit. That I can't do something. I can't save the camp. And I can't save people. Only God can do that. But I *can* love them. God had been teaching me that all week with Madison.

I don't know how much time passed, but Maestro began playing a little louder, and sang a new song.

> *Jesus, you're the one . . .*
> *Who wipes away our tears,*
> *Who gives us hope and love,*
> *Who helps us in our fears.*
> *Jesus, you're the one . . .*
> *There's no one else like You,*

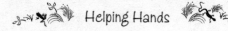

Who rose up from the grave
And makes us all brand new . . .
Jesus, you're the one . . .

"Okay, campers," Bo said softly, "it's time to move. Find another hand that stirs your heart."

I knew just where I wanted to go so I searched for that red-headed girl—the one that I had been trying *so* hard to care for over the last few weeks. And finally, at that moment, I cared about *her* problem more than anything else in the world. So I sprang over to where she had drawn her hand before anyone else could get there. And I read what it said:

My heart hurts because of my parents' divorce.
Help me to forgive them.

And at that moment, my heart broke for Madison Doonsberry. I didn't just feel sorry for her. I didn't just feel sad for her. I felt like I *was* her.

I pressed my hand on hers and prayed. And I cried like I've never cried for another person in my whole life.

CHAPTER 27

Getting Messy

Now, girls, at least make sure you don't get your pillows dirty!" Bliss held the hand sanitizer up in the air while we threw our dirty socks, shoes, candy wrappers, sleeping bags, and blankets all over the place. After our twenty-minute "pig" adventure, we landed on our beds, exhausted—while a few boa feathers floated to the ground.

And then we got the major giggles.

"I didn't realize how much fun being messy could be," Madison said.

"Me either," Ruby said. "Maybe we shouldn't be so hard on the boys."

"I just hope we win the Pig Award," I said. "'Cause there's no way we can be as stinky as them."

More giggles.

"You girls are the *best*," Bliss said. "Three years of prayer really paid off."

An airhorn sounded and we all sat up straight.

"The dinger's gone again!" Madison yelled. And we all popped up and ran down to the box.

"Good morning, campers! Welcome to your last full day at camp! I hope you *all* got a good night's sleep . . ." Johan stared down the group, probably trying to scare last night's dinger

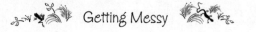

stealers, ". . . because we have our final activity for big points after breakfast."

Madison moved close to me. "What is it? Am I going to get dirty?"

I shook my head. "I don't think so. Wet and slimy, maybe. But only if we don't build it well."

"Build what?"

"Our swamp boat."

Every year, on the last day of camp, we take part in our own little auction—but it's not silent *at all*. It's more like a scream-ing auction. We use our cabin points as money and whoever yells their bid loud enough for Johan to hear gets whatever was up for bid. And in this case, the items are all inflatables— things we can tie together, and then float our whole cabin on, across Bluff Springs Lake—home of the Allibeaver.

Madison was full of questions as we lashed together the giant gorilla, the banana, the rubber raft, and the two floating mats we bought during the scream auction.

"What if we tip over? Or sink? Can we touch the water at all? *Should* we touch the water at all? Are there copperheads in the water?" The terror in her eyes was disturbing.

I grabbed her by the shoulders.

"Madison, everything's going to be okay. The lifeguards are out there in boats. Nobody has ever gotten hurt, bitten, or eaten during the swamp boat competition. Plus, I think we've built a magnificent swamp boat. Check it out!"

I jumped on the banana and bounced up and down. Then I looked over at the boat that Boys' Six was building, and frowned. "I think they're our strongest competition."

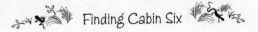

Boys' Six had purchased all the boogie boards and they had tied them together, front to end. And they'd even scored a few paddles!

Johan yelled in the bullhorn, "Cabins, ready? Bring your swamp boats to the north end of the lake. We'll race two at a time, but remember, you are ultimately racing for the best time in the camp. If your boat tips over, you get no points for this event. You will lose a million points for each person that falls totally off the boat. And after that, we will award points based on who was fastest all the way down to slowest. Good luck, and watch out for the Allibeaver! HAHAHAHAHA!"

That's not what Madison needed to hear.

"We got you, Madison," Hayley said. "You and Allie stay in the raft and we'll all be on the sides, paddling."

"Yeah," Shelby added. "We're gonna smoke everyone."

We hauled our boat down to the north end of the lake and checked our tournament pairing. Each cabin had their week-long point total listed on a big dry erase board by the shore. According to tradition, the two cabins with the most points always race against each other in the last heat.

The cabins with the highest points were girls' Cabin Four and boys' Cabin Six.

Great.

"Hey, we know they'll be fast," Ruby said, "so if we can beat *them* we should win it all," I looked at Madison. "If you have any clever ideas, now would be the time to share them."

She shook her head. "Like I said before, I have no deceit left."

The races began. The first two cabins' boats sank. Poor things. With so few points they weren't able to buy many sturdy floats at the auction.

Each race improved just a little. By the third heat most of the campers were able to make it to the other side. In the

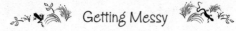

fourth heat the boys' Cabin Five boat broke in two and the halves finished separately.

"We take the time of the last half that finishes," Johan said.

Girls' Cabin Five—the cabin with Lola, Kendall, and their new friends Olivia and Natalie, won their race against boys' Cabin Two. In fact, up to that point, girls' Five had the fastest time.

And then it was our turn.

"I don't think I can do this," Madison said.

Shelby and Julia lifted her up and threw her in the middle of the raft.

Bliss yelled from one of the rescue boats.

"Let's go, God's princesses!"

"Boats ready?" I glanced to the side and saw the boys, each standing next to their boogie boards, ready to launch them into the water.

I *wish they didn't have those paddles.*

Johan held up his airhorn. "On your mark, get set. . . . GO!" The horn blew and we all flew into the swamp.

At first we barely moved, but neither did the boys. Momentum takes a minute to build. But then our gorilla-and-banana swamp boat started making a wake behind us.

"Paddle harder!" Julia yelled, and Kayla and Ashley—who were up front on the mats—dug their arms into the water. Shelby and Hayley held on in the back and kicked as hard as they could. Shelby and Brook did their best from the sides and Madison and I cheered from the middle.

We edged in front of the boys, and then they edged in front of us. At one point I looked over, and Nathan was up on his knees, paddling like crazy.

Hunter brought up the rear of the boogie board chain, so he was behind us. He inched up closer and closer, and then I heard him cheering for us.

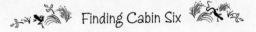

"C'mon, Girls' Four, give us a run for our money!"

And so we did. Swamp water flew everywhere. But when we were about three quarters of the way, the girls started to run out of gas.

"My arms are toast!" Kayla yelled. "I can't paddle anymore!"

"Me too!" Ashley grabbed her shoulder and sat down.

I looked at Madison. "I know you're out of deceit, but do you think you could find some courage and strength?"

She knew exactly what I meant. And she didn't hesitate one second. Madison jumped to the front, and dug her arms into the water, paddling like there was no tomorrow. I joined her, and I could smell certain victory as we neared the shore. The tip of our banana—which stuck out in front of our swamp boat—edged forward, a few inches in front of the boys' boogie boards.

We're gonna win this thing!

Well, at least my thoughts were positive. The outcome was not. I don't know how it happened, but at the last second, a boogie board shot in front of our banana, and shoved into the shore.

Boys' Cabin Six cheered and splashed and high-fived and whooped and hollered. "For Parker! We did it for Parker!"

Well, I couldn't be upset with that.

The Cabin Four girls, with our rubber arms, joined the boys in their celebration. Their victory, added to their week-long point total, would most likely put them in front of us—making them cabin champs.

All the teams gathered on the deck overlooking the lake for the official totals and announcement of the awards. Johan brought his best grumpy face to the ceremony.

"We still have some tallying to do," Johan growled. "Since we had a *three-way* tie for Pig Cabin today! That award that comes with a strenuous S.O.S.—goes to girls' Cabins Four and Five, and boys' Cabin Six."

There was no applause. We didn't dare.

"How do you kids live in such filth?" asked Johan, the guy who never changes his camp clothes.

"And so, you each lose ten million points!"

Yikes. That was harsh.

But the next announcement was epic.

"My time appears to be up. I was NOT able to expose the scoundrels who stole the dinger out of the bell. You may all step forward now, with no fear of consequences."

My head pounded a little. I wasn't sure Johan could be trusted.

But it was tradition, right? So I stepped forward, and Ruby, Kendall, Lola, Madison, Hunter, Nathan, Bliss, and Blaze joined me on the deck.

"Parker came too," I said.

Johan grabbed his thick hair with both hands and pretended to pull it out. "I had a feeling it was all of you—I just didn't have any proof. And Blaze and Bliss, my friends—I'm gonna get you back! The rest of you rascal campers—you get fifty million points for your cabins. But, watch out, you're all on high alert for next year."

If there is a next year.

CHAPTER 28

Special Opportunity to Serve

Our Pig Cabin idea worked. Girls' Cabins Four and Five and boys' Cabin Six were assigned special opportunities to serve at the 50th anniversary gala on Friday evening.

Our arms were tired and sore so most of the kids fought for the job of handing out programs and greeting folks as they came in.

The boys who hadn't bathed since Wednesday's whirlpool were stationed back in the kitchen to scrape plates. They were happy enough with that since they got to eat their fill of pizza back there too.

Lola, Kendall, Ruby, Madison, and I were chosen to push plates of food out on carts and Nathan and Hunter and some of the "cleaner" boys filled water glasses.

Ruby and I served the loudest group in the whole place—the table with Mamaw and her cabinmates. Papaw Ray and Uncle Saul sat at a table next to them.

"They turn into silly high school girls every time they get together," Papaw said, as I placed his plate in front of him.

"They're a spunky bunch!" said Uncle Saul as he picked up his cloth napkin and spread it out on his lap.

The place next to Papaw was empty so I sat down for a moment to have a heart-to-heart talk.

"Papaw, are we really going to let Patterson Gables sell Camp 99 Pines to a housing developer?"

"What do you mean 'we,' sweet pea?"

I leaned in close, so he would hear. "Don't 'we', meaning the Carroway family, have enough money to outbid that developer?"

Uncle Saul chimed in, "Oh, yeah—we got the money, and we could outbid that old Stan all day long. But that'd be *our* way out—not God's way."

"How do you know what God's way is?"

Papaw recited a Bible verse that was familiar. "'The wisdom from above is first of all pure. It is also peace-loving, gentle at all times, and willing to yield to others. It is full of mercy, and good deeds. It shows no favoritism and it is always sincere.' That's James 3:17."

There's that word again. Mercy.

"Okay. I think I get it. Instead of fighting with Patterson Gables, we're supposed to be peaceful and respect him even if he doesn't deserve it?"

Papaw patted me on the shoulder. "God'll soften him up, you'll see."

"You know," Uncle Saul added, "Patterson was in our cabin the very first year 99 Pines was open. He used to love this place. He even helped us save the camp from . . ."

Papaw pushed a roll in Saul's mouth before he could finish his sentence.

"Allie-girl, I think you've got some dinners on that cart to deliver." Papaw Ray got up and pulled my chair out for me to stand.

"Thanks, Papaw. I'm sorry there isn't room for you to sit next to Mamaw tonight."

He laughed. "I don't want to sit next to a bunch of crazy camp women. I'll do just fine over here, thanks."

I smiled. "Okay, I'll be back in a little while with your dessert."

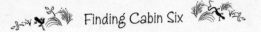
And then I ran off with the cart to go find my cousins.

I grabbed Hunter by the sleeve and dragged him over to the corner of the tent. "Stay right here while I get the girls." He was munching on a roll, so he was fine with that.

I spotted Lola a few tables over and I waved her over.

"What's up?"

"I have a new piece of information to share. You get Ruby and I'll find Kendall. Meet us over where Hunter is, in that corner. Hurry!"

In less than a minute, my cousins and I were all huddled together under the corner of the lighted tent.

"You guys, I just found out that Patterson Gables helped save the camp the first year. If he did it once, he could do it again!"

"What do you want us to do, Allie? I'll do anything. You want me to put a frog in his cheesecake?" Kendall laughed.

I shook my head. "There's nothing *we* can do. But we can sure ask God to do something. We've got a whole tent full of people who love this camp and I bet all of them together have enough money to buy it. But God's gotta soften Patterson Gables' heart first."

We put our heads together and said a prayer for all that to happen.

Hunter patted his chest with his open hand. "God's gonna do it, Allie. I can feel it."

And then we went back to delivering dinners to the few remaining people, all the while being peace-loving, sincere, and hopeful.

The program was about to begin.

Lindsey Roth, all dressed up in a green beaded, floor-length gown, approached the podium. As she did, the live band that was playing over in the corner faded out.

"Good evening, Camp 99 Pines alumni. We are privileged to have you here to celebrate 50 years of camping, laughing, crying, and caring. Tonight is all about you, and the blessing you have been to this place. We want to start the celebration with a video—50 Years at 99 Pines."

The lights dimmed and the presentation began. It was a mix of lively music, pictures, and video, and as Madison pointed out, it looked like nothing had changed at the camp over the years. Activities, places, campfire talks—the only thing that was different in all those scenes was the people. Several pictures of my aunts, uncles, and mom and dad popped up—playing tug-o'war, participating in the whirl-pool, and running with Frisbees. There was even a picture of Mamaw holding up the bell dinger and smiling. And there was a guy standing next to her who looked kinda familiar. Was that Papaw Ray?

When that picture showed up, the whole crowd cheered.

I scoped the room for Patterson Gables. He was sitting toward the front of the room eating his dinner, his body facing away from the screen. He was having a discussion with that Stan guy. But Stan wasn't eating. He was gesturing wildly and shaking his head. Then he got up and walked toward where we were standing at the back.

"Hello, sir," I said. I cleared my throat. "Can I get you something?"

He squinted down at me in the dim light. "Allie Carroway? Oh, hello. Thank you for the offer, but I don't need anything."

I grinned. "Okay."

"But Patterson Gables needs something."

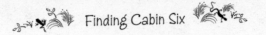

"Oh?" I looked over at his table. "Is he out of water? Salad dressing?"

Stan shook his head. "No. He's out a buyer for this camp. I'm not going to build houses here. You all are building something much more valuable."

He held out his hand to shake mine. "God bless you all." And then he walked from the tent out into the darkness.

Adrenaline squirted through my veins and I rose on my tiptoes to try to locate Miss Lindsey. It didn't take long for me to find her. She was up at the podium again.

"Wasn't that fun? Thank you to all who contributed pictures and video. And now, I would like to ask anyone who made a commitment to the Lord while at Camp 99 Pines to please stand up and come to the podium. Say your name, and the year you made the commitment—if you can remember!"

Gasps traveled through the audience as more than half the guests stood up. I glanced over at Patterson. His body and face were still turned away from the front.

As names were being announced, Mamaw made her way back to me. She wiped tears from the corners of her eyes with a napkin.

"Are you okay, Mamaw?"

She put her hand on my head. "Yes, I am more than okay. This is just so happy and sad at the same time. We need this camp for future generations. We almost lost it once and if we had, all these people might not have found the Lord."

"How did you almost lose it? And how was it saved?"

And then I decided to spill the beans.

"Mamaw, I know that the Prayer Barn on your property is girls' Cabin Six."

Mamaw's eyes got big and her mouth dropped open.

"I can't even believe I'm asking you this, but . . . did you and your cabinmates steal Cabin Six?"

Mamaw was silent for a minute, as names echoed in the background.

Finally, she turned, and put both hands on my shoulders.

"No, Allie. We didn't steal Cabin Six. We sold it! At a 'silent' silent auction the last night of camp—to help raise the insurance money. Your Papaw Ray and Uncle Saul's father bought it, and all of us girls in Cabin Six, with the help of Patterson, Ray, and Saul, loaded it on a flatbed trailer so they could haul it away in the middle of the night. We told everyone that it was a prank—kinda like stealing the dinger—and then over the years, people made up stories about its disappearance . . ."

"*Sold it*? But how can you sell something that doesn't belong to you?"

"Well, it belonged to someone in our cabin."

"Who?"

"Goldie."

"Goldie? Your *counselor*?"

At that moment, thunderous applause filled the tent. Lindsey Roth wheeled in an elderly woman in a wheelchair. Her white hair looked stunning with her silver necklace and royal blue chiffon dress. When she reached the podium, Lindsey helped her stand, and she stayed next to her—holding her up—as the audience grew still and the woman spoke.

"Hello, friends."

There was a long pause while the woman looked like she was trying to gather her thoughts.

"Thank you for . . . being here. I . . ."

More silence. She shook her head and Lindsey reassured her.

"It's okay, Miss Audrey. You can sit now. We're just so glad *you're* here."

Audrey? Could this be *Audrey Gables*?

But Miss Audrey didn't want to sit. She shook her head and

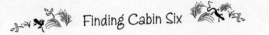

then continued. "Do not worry . . . about the future . . . of the camp . . ."

That got Patterson to finally turn around. Audrey looked straight at him.

"I . . . love you, son. And . . . I know . . . you'll do the right thing." Then, her eyes cleared and she straightened up. "For I know the one in whom I trust, and I am sure that he is able to guard what I have entrusted to him until the day of his return."

Mamaw sighed. "Second Timothy 1:12. That's always been Goldie's favorite verse."

"Goldie?"

Mamaw nodded. "Goldie is Audrey's camp name."

Goldie's speech ended with a standing ovation, and immediately following that we girls were supposed to serve cheesecake. We tried, but no one was sitting in their seats. Instead, they were huddled in groups, buzzing about Patterson Gables.

"His buyer dropped out," I overheard someone say. "This is our chance."

"Does the board have enough money to make an offer?"

"Where can I make a donation?"

"Anybody seen Lindsey?"

People crowded the silent auction tables like they were deals on Black Friday. I wiggled my way to one of the tables and saw that my camo jacket from season one of *Carried Away with the Carroways* was in the middle of a bidding war. I jumped over to another table where one item seemed to have the longest line of bidders. I squeezed in, and couldn't believe what I saw.

It was the dinger from the bell! And it was bringing in *lots* of bucks.

I glanced behind the table and saw Bliss pointing to the bid sheet and giving her Aunt Betsy a high-five.

Those rascals. Bliss stole the dinger twice in one week!

I located Lindsey Roth engaged in what looked like a serious discussion with Mamaw and some of the Cabin Six ladies over at their table. They obviously needed cheesecake, so I found a cart and flew over there.

As I served them, I heard Betsy say, "Are we anywhere close to the asking price?"

Lindsey shook her head. "Not yet. We need a miracle."

"Another Bless-ception, perhaps?" Mamaw asked.

"A what?" Lindsey asked.

Mamaw grabbed her by the arm. "Follow me."

CHAPTER 29

Good News and Goodbyes

And, just like that, our week at camp was over. The airhorn blew, signaling our last breakfast—cinnamon rolls and bacon—a meal that everyone loves but has trouble choking down because of being all choked up.

"This has been my favorite week, ever!" Bliss popped out of bed and gave us each a little jewelry box with a pink heart charm in it. "I will never forget you girls."

Tears began flowing everywhere. I tried to change the subject since there were no tissues left.

"You were out late last night, Bliss," I said. And I raised an eyebrow. "You were out late the night before too."

Bliss stretched and yawned. "Yes, and I'm sorry. I hope Ember checked in on you. I've been on some . . . adventures . . . with my Aunt Betsy."

Madison sat up on her top bunk, her legs dangling down. "I miss my puppy, and my home, but now I feel like our princess palace is home too. I'm glad I came." She jumped down and came over to give me a hug. "Allie, thanks for putting up with me. I know I haven't been the easiest person to be around. I don't know what I would have done without your help and support all week."

"It was my pleasure, Madison."

Madison stepped back and raised an eyebrow. "Really?"

"Okay, maybe not at first."

Madison grinned. "I could tell. But I don't blame you. After all I did to you . . ."

I put my hand out.

"Nuh-uh. You're forgiven, remember? And, hey—maybe when I get moved into my new house, you could, you know, come over. And bring Petunia."

Madison crunched her eyebrows together. "You mean to hang out? As friends?"

I smiled. "Sure, why not? That's what we are, right?"

Madison let out a big sigh. "Well, you tend to bond with a person when you're shoved under a building with them for half a night." Then she smiled and held out her hand to shake mine. "Friends."

Bliss sniffled in the background but then came over with a squirt of hand sanitizer for the both of us. "Three years of praying. See? I knew this year would be special."

We packed up, put our luggage outside our cabins, and headed down to the box. There was a whole lot of buzz going on down there.

"Allie!" Hunter ran over and tugged on my sleeve. "Cabin Six has vanished!"

"I know that, silly. It's been gone for a long time. Zola's still out there, looking for the last camper."

"No. I'm talking about *boys'* Cabin Six! We slept overnight in the treehouse, and we returned to just a concrete slab! Good thing we had all our stuff with us, or the pranksters would have gotten away with my dinosaur pillowcase!"

Boys' Cabin Six? Gone?

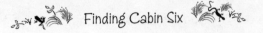

"Attention, campers!" Someone really needed to get Johan a new shirt. "We have a special guest this morning to say grace. Please give a warm welcome to our Camp Director, Miss Lindsey Roth."

We applauded loudly. Then Miss Lindsey took the bullhorn. "This is a very good morning, and I have some great news. Late last night, the governing board of Camp 99 Pines made an offer to buy the camp from Patterson Gables and he accepted. We'll be signing the papers this afternoon, as soon as you all are checked out."

"Yeah," Johan added. "So hurry up and get outta here!"

Cheers erupted and kids stormed the top of the box to high-five Miss Lindsey.

Johan got back on the bullhorn. "Get down, you rowdies! You're messin' up my shirt."

We got down. And then Miss Lindsey prayed.

"Thank you, Lord, for your many blessings, but most of all, thank you for giving us new life in Jesus Christ. Be with everyone as they return home today and keep them safe all year. Encourage those who made first-time commitments to you here at Camp 99 Pines, and help us all to remember there is no problem too big for you to handle. We love you. In Jesus' name, amen."

Then we ended with our last Doxology of the week:

> *Praise God from whom all blessings flow;*
> *Praise Him all creatures here below;*
> *Praise Him above, ye Heavenly Host;*
> *Praise Father, Son, and Holy Ghost. Amen.*

It was a sweet sound, with all the kids singing. But the best voice, the loudest one, singing every word this morning, belonged to Madison Doonsberry.

188

"Can I help you with those bags?"

Nathan Fremont was standing at the tree. The one right in front of the girls' village. The one where he dropped me off at the beginning of the week.

I smiled. "Hi."

I put my suitcase down.

He smiled. "Hi."

Those dimples . . . again.

"How did you like Jesus Swamp Camp?"

"It was the best week of my life—except for the Parker snake-bite thing."

"I'm glad you didn't get eaten by an alligator."

"My cabin got stolen though."

"But you were cabin champs."

Nathan laughed. "Yeah. It was also the *weirdest* week of my life."

"That's how things go in the bayou."

"Then I kinda like the bayou." Nathan grabbed the handle of my suitcase. "Can I take this to your car?"

I shrugged. "In a minute." Then I sighed to myself. "I owe you a headlamp."

I set my suitcase on the ground and unzipped it. Then I reached in the netted pouch and pulled out both—the pink one and the brown camo.

"I guess they're kinda tangled together." I held them out to Nathan. "Do you mind?" I knew I wouldn't be able to unknot them with my jittery, clammy fingers while he watched.

"Sure."

Nathan worked a minute, and soon the two headlamps

were separated. I held out my hand and waited for him to give me the pink one. He started to hand it over, but then . . . he gave me the brown one instead.

"I was thinking," he said and looked down at the ground and then back up at me. "Would you mind keeping . . . *my* head-lamp . . . until . . . next time?"

"Next time?" I fidgeted. And I suddenly felt like I needed ten puffs from my inhaler.

"Yeah, next time. And I'll keep yours—*if* that's okay."

Say something, Allie. And whatever you do, don't faint.

I grinned and reached out for the beat-up brown headlamp with MATT 51415 scrawled on the strap.

My most prized possession.

"No, Dude. I don't mind at all."

CHAPTER 30

Timbuktu

Moving day had finally arrived. I held the keys in my hand! Carroway trucks filled with boxes and furniture lined the street, and all my uncles, aunts, cousins, my dad and mom—followed me as I opened the door to our brand-new house on Timbuktu Court. Camera crews were there too—to film an episode of *Carried Away with the Carroways* entitled *Moving to Timbuktu*.

"Take a breath, girl!" Dad smiled. "That's an entryway free of allergens."

I breathed in deep. And then I sneezed, which caused laughter to erupt throughout the whole group.

You can bet that'll be in the show.

"I'm sure I still have camp dirt up my nose," I said.

"Let's go check out the backyard!" Hunter yelled.

Aunt Kassie put her hand out. "Not yet, bucko. First, everyone takes at least three boxes to the correct rooms. And we labeled them all, so no guessing."

Our dogs ran through our legs and barked as we formed a train of moving boxes. And once we got started, we just kept going until Mamaw Kat, Papaw Ray, and Uncle Saul pulled up with lunch.

"Who needs food?" Mamaw carried a pot of something that smelled yummy into the house.

"Lunch break!" Our director, Zeke, put down his clipboard and went to help Mamaw with her pot. "Best food in Louisiana has arrived."

Papaw and Uncle Saul brought in more pots and casserole dishes of food and baskets of bread—and pies. They spread them out on our huge, new kitchen island.

Dad came in from the backyard. "We set up some portable tables outside, so let's pray in here and then go out and enjoy a little fresh air before we haul in the furniture."

Uncle Wayne groaned. "Aww, you don't need furniture, do ya?"

My whole family circled up, along with the film crew, Zeke, and our wardrobe manager, Hannah.

"Try not to slop gumbo on your clothes," she said.

"Allie," Dad said. "Would you like to say the first blessing in our new house?"

I tried to swallow the big lump that had formed in my throat.

"Yes, I would."

Everyone bowed their heads. And then a bunch of thoughts bombarded my mind all at once. The last nine months had seemed so long, but flew by at the same time. This time last year, Hunter wasn't even part of the family yet. And we still had that old, moldy clubhouse—the Diva Duck Blind. I even thought my family was going to have to move to Arizona because of my allergies.

Thank you, Lord, that you had a better plan.

"Is something wrong Allie-gator?" Dad was smiling, and now everyone's head was up and looking at me.

"No, not at all. Everything is really good."

So, I prayed.

"Father, thank you. For my family. For my home. For everything you provide. For working in my life. For showing me how to love people. But most of all, thank you for Jesus, and for the promise of heaven. Bless this food, and bless the people around this circle. In Jesus' name, amen."

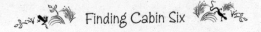

"Hey, what's that?" As we piled out the back door, Hunter pointed to a wooden building that sat up on blocks out on the large parcel of land behind our pool.

"That's my new duck blind," Dad said.

It was no duck blind.

I shaded my eyes with my hand. "Is that what I think it is?"

"Okay, it's not a duck blind. Surprise! I thought you might like to have your very own Prayer Barn." Dad came over and patted me on the shoulder. "I know how much you like the one at Mamaw's house."

"That ain't a duck blind, and it ain't a Prayer Barn." Uncle Saul smiled. "That there is a bless-ception!"

I shoved my hands on my hips.

"Wait just a minute, people. I heard Mamaw use that term at the gala. What's a bless-ception?"

"A bless-ception," Papaw Ray said, "is a blessing, disguised as a deception."

"That can't be a thing," Kendall said.

"Oh, it's a *Carroway* thing," Mom said. "Kat, Ray, and Saul invented it way back when they helped Audrey Gables sell girls' Cabin Six. The money from that sale gave them the last bit of money they needed to pay the insurance, and it *blessed* the camp. But they decided to make up a story . . . a deception . . ."

"Because it's *camp*!" Kendall hit it right on the nose.

Mamaw laughed. "Well, yes. Everyone loves a little mystery at camp, right? But, Audrey wanted us to keep the sale of the cabin a secret. You see, when they came up a little short of funds after the silent auction, Audrey knew that her husband Quincy would be too proud to ask people to give even more.

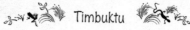

But, she was a spunky one, and she was determined to keep Camp 99 Pines open."

"I wonder if she ever told Quincy where that last bit of money came from?"

Mamaw came over and put her hand on my shoulder. "I don't know, Allie-girl. But we can go visit her and ask. I'm sure she'll remember every detail of that story, and she'd probably love to tell it, after all these years."

I smiled. "I'd love to."

Hunter scratched his head. "Is *that* boys' Cabin Six out there?"

Uncle Saul laughed. "Remember when I told you kids that God would stop all that camp sale nonsense? Well, I was right, wasn't I? And we *might* have held another 'silent' silent auction last night, after the gala. But y'all better go see for yourself!"

Hunter, Kendall, Lola, Ruby, and I ditched our full plates of food and ran toward the wooden building. We had to step up to get to the door. I climbed in first, and then reached back for Kendall. Everyone else followed.

The cabin still had the bunks and mattresses in it. Five, in all. Two going down the long walls and one in the back on the short wall. And they had the same window configuration as all the other cabins, including Mamaw's Prayer Barn.

Hunter climbed up to the top of the bunk to the left of the door. He lay down and stared at the ceiling. "Yep, this is Cabin Six. There's a pattern of wood knots on the ceiling that looks like a Stegosaurus. Check it out! I looked at that thing all week." He showed us the wood knots, but we couldn't make out a Stegosaurus.

"Where did Parker sleep?" Kendall asked, and we all groaned.

"Right below me," Hunter said. And Kendall sat down on the mattress.

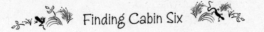
"And Nathan slept right across from him, over there on the right lower bunk."

Thanks for that fun bit of information, Hunter!

"I'm glad Parker's going to be alright," Kendall said. "That was one of the scariest moments ever."

"We've survived a lot of scary moments over the last few months. How about when Ruby almost got eaten by the gator? And when we dropped the water balloons to catch the Hollywoodlum? And when I accidentally ate that peanut?"

"And when we thought you were moving to Arizona?" Kendall put her hand to her cheek.

Lola shivered. "That was the *worst*. The Carroway cousins need to stay together—forever."

"I'm all for that," I said. "I need you people in my life."

"Let's make a deal," Kendall said. "That even when we grow up and get married, we'll live in the same neighborhood, and raise our kids here. Just think, they can meet in the Lickety Split clubhouse, we can tell them all our scary survival stories, and we can keep secrets about bless-ceptions so they can solve the mystery of the missing cabins."

"Sounds like a deal to me," Ruby said.

"Let's stack hands on it." Hunter jumped down from his bunk.

"Okay, Carroway cousins forever, on three," I said.

We put our hands in the circle.

"One, two, three . . . Carroway cousins forever!"

"Hey," I said. "We should go check the back of the cabin to make sure it has a circle with a B6 in the middle of it."

"I'm on it!" Hunter yelled, and he ran out the door with Kendall, Ruby, and Lola following close behind.

I, however, stayed back. I wanted to take a minute to look around and thank God for my new Prayer Barn.

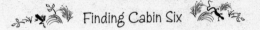

This whole nine months has been crazy, God. Thanks for being with me through it all.

I decided to sit on Nathan's bed. I couldn't help myself. The mattress was the lumpiest thing ever!

Poor guy slept on this all week? He may never come back!

I pulled the mattress down on the floor to check for holes. Maybe his bed had been broken too.

Nope. All boards were intact. Just an old lumpy mattress.

As I reached down to pull it back up on the wood frame, something caught my eye.

Letters had been carved into the frame.

I took my index finger and ran it over the fresh carvings. And my heart skipped a few beats when I figured out what it said:

NF (B6)

AC (G4)

And there was a heart drawn in the middle.

NF ♥ AC.

Nathan Fremont loves Allie Carroway?

I put my hand over my heart, and my cheeks heated up.

Well, Nathan Fremont, California Surfer Dude, if this is true, I hope you don't mind living in the Louisiana Bayou someday with a princess in camo and a bunch of her cousins.

Because I just made a deal.

Let's see where the Princess in Camo series all began! Here's an excerpt from book one,

Allie's Bayou Rescue

CHAPTER 1

Change-up

A llie, we need to talk. Some things are about to change around here!"

Mom pulled a stool out from our kitchen island and patted the red plaid cushion for me to come and sit down. But hearing the word "change" stirred up my stomach and made me feel more like throwing up. Or doing a triple-backflip. Sometimes, when I get real nervous, I triple-flip and then throw up.

But Mom was smiling, so this had to be a *good* change, right?

I edged my way to the stool, and tried to think about the very best change that could possibly happen to me.

"Did my latest allergy tests come back? Can I eat nuts now without having my tongue swell up to the size of a bullfrog?" That would be awesome. Just to have one "death food" off my list of, well . . . too many.

Mom put her hand on my shoulder.

"No, honey, you're still allergic. The tests did come back,

though, and we might have found what's causing your asthma attacks."

Panic shot from my stomach to my throat.

Please don't say pasta. Please don't say pasta. Please don't say pasta.

Mom scrunched up her nose.

"It looks like mold's a suspect."

"Mold?" I threw my hands up in the air. "That's just great. We live in Floodsville, USA."

"Yes, I know. And we'll have to work something out about that. But don't you worry about it at all. For now, let's talk about the *big* news of the day."

"Wait. Are you telling me that the big news of the day is *bigger* than finding out that living in Louisiana could kill me at any moment?"

Mom pulled out a stool and sat down. "Well, when you put it like that, no. But Louisiana is *not* going to kill you. We'll work it out, you'll see."

I hopped up on the stool next to her, swallowed hard, and gripped the cushion to hold on tight.

You can handle this, Allie. Whatever it is.

I took a deep breath and blew it out.

"Okay, give me the news. I'm ready."

Mom's blue eyes popped open wider than usual, and she slapped the counter.

"You're getting a new cousin!"

Another cousin? Well, that didn't seem like huge news at all. My dad has three brothers who are married to women who tend to have babies from time to time.

Mold seemed to be a bigger deal. But I pretended to go along with the excitement anyway.

"Who's pregnant this time? Aunt Janie?"

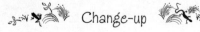

Mom shook her head.

"Aunt Kassie?"

"No."

"Well, Aunt Lorraine's a little older, but that would make for an interesting TV episode."

"Allie!"

"I'm just saying . . ."

My whole family stars in a reality TV show called *Carried Away with the Carroways*. For some reason, millions of people are interested in how all my uncles, aunts, grandparents, and cousins live in the Louisiana Bayou. I have a hard time understanding the fascination, because it's just something I've always known. And to be honest, I think we can be a little boring at times. Most days are spent filming what's going on around here—just us, living out our regular lives. It's kinda nuts. But at least not the kind of nuts that will cause me to stop breathing.

Mom leaned in close to me, and pushed my long, dark-blonde hair back behind one ear.

"Allie, nobody's pregnant. Kassie and Wayne are adopting Hunter!"

Now, if we had been filming a Carroway TV episode at that very moment—this is where the editors would have added the "dun, dun, dun," music into the scene.

Hunter . . . *is going to become a Carroway?*

Hunter?

Mom nudged my shoulder.

"Allie, isn't that exciting?"

I held onto that cushion with all my might to keep from bolting.

"Um . . . yes, ma'am." I tried not to make eye contact, but Mom wasn't having it.

"Well, you don't look too excited." She reached over and

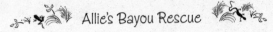

pulled down on my cheek with her thumb. "And your eyes are all glazed over. What did you eat for lunch?"

I shrugged.

"Mac and cheese." It's a good thing I'm not allergic to dairy or wheat, or I'd starve to death.

"Then why do you look so pale?" Mom put her hand on my forehead and scrunched her eyebrows together. "How's your breathing?"

I breathed in, held it, and then blew out. I wondered for a moment if this mold issue could get me out of filming TV episodes in the swamp.

"I'm good," I said, but I'm sure my fidgeting was giving me away. "Just trying to process the news."

Mom pulled her hand back and tilted her head to the side. One eyebrow shot up a little.

"Hey, I know you don't love change. And I know that Hunter can be a little rowdy at times."

"That's not a problem. Kendall's way rowdier than Hunter."

Kendall is my thirteen-year-old cousin who always sings at the top of her lungs. She's the daughter of Kassie and Wayne, so after the adoption, that would make her Hunter's sister. And *that* would make for a loud household.

Mom continued. "And I know he can be messy."

"Nope, Lola's got him beat. Have you ever seen her room? You could hide Ruby's entire preschool Sunday school class in her clothes piles."

Lola and Ruby are also my cousins, ages eleven and ten. They're the daughters of my Uncle Josiah and Aunt Janie. You'd never know they're sisters. They don't look a thing alike and their personalities are the exact opposite.

"Okay then." Mom laughed a little. "I will admit, Hunter goes a little overboard in his collecting of reptiles for pets."

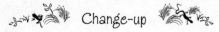

I crossed my arms *and* rolled my eyes.

"Mom, reptiles *swarm* this place. I'm glad he catches some to keep them from crawling all over me."

Mom slid off her stool, walked around the kitchen island, and opened the refrigerator door. She poured a glass of iced tea and took a sip.

"Then I don't understand, Allie. What's the problem?"

The truth is—I love Hunter. He's funny and smart, and I love his big laugh. Sometimes he uses complicated words that I have to look up. But my vocabulary grades have been improving because of it. I'd been praying for him to find a loving family ever since Kassie and Wayne took him in as a foster child a couple of months earlier.

But . . . there *was* a problem. A big one.

"Allie, I asked you a question."

Mom's eyes narrowed. She put one hand on her hip, and with the other she shook her cup, rattling the ice cubes.

I struggled to pull myself out of the twilight zone.

"I'm sorry. I'm really happy for everyone."

"Then why do you look like you just whiffed fish guts?"

"I do *not* look like that. Really, everything's fine."

I tried to slip off the stool and run away, but Mom grabbed me by the shoulder.

"Allie Kate, you will stay put until we finish this conversation." When she whips out "Allie Kate," she means business.

I scooted back up to the middle of the stool and put on my serious face.

"Yes, ma'am. What was the question again?"

"What's the problem with Hunter becoming a Carroway?"

It appeared there was no getting out of it, so I tried to explain.

"Well," I sighed. "You know how all us cousins hang out all the time?"

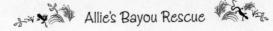

"Of course. You can hardly avoid it. You work together, go to school together, live within shouting distance of each other . . ."

"Yes."

I opened my left hand and spread the fingers out to count on them.

"And there's me, Kendall, Lola, and Ruby."

I ticked off all four fingers, leaving the thumb without a name.

"Yes, but you have a bunch of other cousins too."

"But they're either a lot younger or a lot older. I'm talking about the ones who are the same age. Me, Kendall, Lola, and Ruby."

I ticked my fingers again.

"Okay, yeah."

"Well, now we're getting one more in the same age group."

Mom stared down at my fingers.

"That seems perfect. It'll make a whole hand full of cousins." She laughed.

I made a fist. The fingers all folded in together, and the thumb, well—it stuck out. No matter what I did with it, it just didn't seem to fit in. And there was only one reason for it.

This was going to be a challenge.

"Mom, the problem is . . . Hunter's a boy."